Electric Flesh

Electric Flesh

by Claro

Translation by Brian Evenson

Soft Skull Press
Brooklyn 2006

Published by
Soft Skull Press
55 Washington St, Suite 804
Brooklyn NY 11201
www.softskull.com

Distributed by Publishers Group West
1.800.788.3123 www.pgw.com

Printed in Canada.

Design by Alexandra Escamilla

44Library of Congress Cataloging-in-Publication Data

Claro, Christophe, 1962-
[Chair électrique. English]
Electric flesh / Claro ; translation by Brian Evenson.
p. cm.
ISBN 1-933368-23-3
I. Evenson, Brian, 1966- II. Title.

PQ2663.L287C4313 2006
843'.914--dc22

2006004046

And now swallow your law.
—Artaud

For Marion

discontinuous memories of the besieged current

If it were an animal, it would be a baboon, a raw rage, a gnarled fury ready to snap at the least caress, but it isn't an animal, it's only a date—date or disaster, same difference, same water brought to various degrees of boiling or ignorance, it's what unties tongues when they thicken, it's what rouses rats when they come aboard, it's the 7th of August 1881, the year when President Garfield is shot, when the leading dinosaurs (*brontosaurus amplus*) are christened, when the great Pop Smith plays for the Buffalo Bisons, and in fact this takes place in Buffalo, not far from Niagara Falls (in Indian: *Onguiaahra,* "straits"), it is near 11 p.m. and George L. Smith, 31 years old, dockworker by trade & alcoholic by choice, following-up on a not very bright bet with his brother Vince, tries to couple with the Brush Electric Light Company generator, located on Ganson Street.

Said generator doesn't flaunt particularly exciting curves: it's a stupefied pachyderm, kneeling in its own power, overhauled in a rush and as a result quite prone to outages.

George steps forward, titillated by the regular purring of the generator, which is dreaming about curdling all his molecules. The thing gapes, parts its silky and rusty skirts, arches its back. The energy emitted is such that any resistance makes it immediately increase. It's a remarkable moment: when desire treats ridicule with disdain in order to return to its forbidden roots, where to bend is to become an arc, no matter the arrows, no matter the target, blood becomes bone, bone bends, *tschaaak!* Hardly has George placed his callous-ridden paws on the zinc friction plates (first the right—tinglings—then the left—*zrrip! ting!*), than his entire mental & emotional system is absorbed and dissolved, his balls shrink to become knucklebones in a geezer's fist, the puddled cry that he's about to retch out dries at the rim of his nostrils, the temperature of his bladder climbs in a half second to 95 degrees, his vision inverts, all his memories are reduced to the size of the head of a pin which sinks without jolts or hesitation into the deliquescent marrow of his urges—the ill-bound scrapbook of his life explodes fanlike and pollinates his last moments, he rethinks, resees, reneges, at once extremely volatile and overcome by gravity for good, *schomp! schomp! schomp!* leaden images strike his hide—at random: the surprised face of his mother, a glove between her thighs, the taste of maple sap while staying in Montreal, a barber's flickering sign in the early hours of September when he came back fully intoxicated after a prolonged immersion in the land of venal pleasures, a fingernail once torn off when he lifted a 99 lb. crate, all that, all those things not worth recording but worthy only of being forgotten are instantaneously mixed ground tamped down then melted into a hard point, tempered by the moment of death, simultaneously galvanized and annihilated. The constellation George L. Smith has just entered its nothingness phase. *Paralysis of the nerves of respiration*, concludes coroner Joseph Fowler the next day, performing an autopsy at the authority's request. The heart was stopped as suddenly as a union activist beneath the convincing blow of a billy club. There apparently wasn't any "pain"—

> *(and that the pain must be rather incredible to not be apparent, that the body strives to give no evidence of it, muscular or otherwise, that's what starts one thinking, and what makes of this thought an even more abominable pain)*

The aforementioned Smith has just inaugurated the litany of the Great Toasted of Pan-Electric History. Without knowing, he attains the rank of pioneer of the new American frontier, which will tame continuous current and imprison the wild West of bodies in a reservation under voltametrical surveillance.

Here's where the Great Extractor intervenes . . .

ADVERTISEMENT:

"TREMBLE, OH TENDER GUMS, AND YOU MEDIOCRE MOLARS, FOR YOUR PATRON SAINT HAS JUST WALKED INTO THE PATENT SHOP. THE MAKER OF CROWNS, THE ENCRUSTER OF FILLINGS SEES HIS REIGN BEGIN."

He's a dentist, called Alfred Porter Southwick, and when at breakfast he falls upon coroner Fowler's report, when he savors its barbecue-prose ("exceedingly uncommon detail, the brains were cooked"), he senses that his fate of being a stump puller is about to undergo an unexpected revolution. Southwick, so so so, declares out of the blue that electricity, toyed with at low voltage, could:

> *1) Replace Anesthetic during medical operations;*
> *2) become a form of Euthanasia for all unwanted stray animals falling under the responsibility of the city.*

Affixing his silver forceps onto the twin foreheads of his two newborn girls, wild Euthanasia and bitch Anesthesia, the former dentist becomes de facto the wicked stepmother of the unwanted—beasts first, then men. He organizes a crusade the way others launch a subscription, and treats himself to the help of two wicked fairies, Dr. George E. Fell, zealous electrotherapist, inventor of the "Fell Motor" (a pulmonary reanimator which we have nothing to do with here, and certainly not elsewhere), and Colonel Rockwell, president of the Buffalo Society of the Prevention of Cruelty to Animals. These three men, whom even a sexual deviance wouldn't have been enough to bring together, throw themselves into a series of experiments on stray dogs and cats which could no longer decently be drowned in the river. An alcoholic dockworker understood how to properly bow out—if one didn't dwell too long on the burns on his palms and his gray matter being brought to a white heat—so it should be possible to eliminate likewise all four-legged criminals from the street.

Agreement of tenses and empathy of places: the opponents of capital punishment, hostile to the gibbet and anxious to finally give pain a reasonable Richter scale, these defenders of vertical dignity raise their voices, hoist them, even, up to the skies & to the judges' doorsteps. A current of opinion starts to quiver through the great democratic soup: hangings, often (and because) slapdash, start giving off with the help of press and attorneys a medieval whiff, which immediately perfumes the pathetic concept of pathetic progress. Just as one right can cut across another only if each finds pleasure and interest in that bisection, so a certain MacMillan, sidekick to Southwick, advances the hypothesis according to which a painless death will nail shut the capital-punishment-abolishers' traps. MacMillan, whose wife has just perished, drowned in a slurry pit, MacMillan who his contemporaries describe as a "spat-out seed coming back to haunt the idea of the fruit which it pitted"—which says quite a lot about his maturity—consults Governor David Bennett Hill, who very quickly makes a proposal to the Legislature aiming to replace the gallows with electricity. A commission is set underway:

The Death Commission[1]

Whose purpose is, let's cite & savor, "to study and to bring to public awareness the most humane and most effective method there is to successfully complete the execution of the death sentence."

Southwick, of course, the necessary abcess in the humanitarian maw, is named as primary expert along with two other members, two bold, barking switch-flickers by the names of Matthew Hale and Elbridge T. Gerry. A man of law doubling as a brilliant orator, Hale will know how to sort out legal difficulties. Gerry is the founder of the American Society for the Prevention of Cruelty to Animals and to Children (but not to cadavers). A 95 page report inventorying all past and present forms of individual extermination is written up—forced labor unfortunately doesn't appear therein, nor does sexual abstinence or electioneering. A 5-point questionnaire, mentioning electrocution, is sent to hundreds of experts of every sex (as long as they're male). Responses rush in, numerous, nearly two hundred. A certain Dr. Brill, originally of New York City, assesses that since lightning doesn't kill at every strike, it is useless to expect anything from electricity; J. Henry Furman, of Tarrytown, proposes a metallic chair whose legs rest in a zinc solution; Alfred Carroll, of New Brighton, is also inclined in favor of electricity,

1. DC, as in Direct Current, Divine Comedy, Double Collision, Dominating Carnally, Dismembered Character, Danse Coupable . . . Don't Come!

because according to him the gallows no longer have any dissuasive power, they even have a certain prestige, a folkloric aura which urges the criminal to inscribe himself into the grim legend, it's a platform, a stage, a fucking podium! Professor Elihu Thompson estimates the cost of a lethal battery at two hundred dollars maximum and commits to mass-produce them.

As for Thomas Alva Edison, he is content with sending a letter to Southwick on the 8th of November 1887 to remind him that he is opposed to capital punishment and is a believer in reincarnation. But on the 9th of the following December, Edison drafts a second letter, in which he writes: "The most suitable apparatus for the purpose is that class of dynamo-electric machinery which employs alternating currents, manufactured principally in this country by George Westinghouse." Edison, the apostle of the continuous, immediately proposes the alternating, the spearhead of his direct competitor, George Westinghouse, because he understands that by associating discontinuous current and capital punishment, he is damaging his rival: who would dare invite into his house the executioner's lights? And here's Edison working the strings from a hardly clearer shadow and managing to acquire an alternating current generator, under the very nose of his hated rival. He throws himself body & bucks into a series of wild experiments, grilling dogs, cats, horses, elephants, before presenting to the Death Commission his model *made in holy wood*, the First Electric Chair, the very one which will roast the murderer William Kemmler on the 6th of August 1890 at the Auburn prison.

aborted escapology attempt

Another date other facts another life—another name, also: Howard Hordinary. It is Saturday the 14th of August 1996. It is exactly 7:28 p.m., *tixit* the living room wall clock. The adventures of Southwick & Co., the slaughtered baboons on the assembly line, the battle of currents, the first human barbecues in Auburn or Sing-Sing Prison, Howard knows it all, and for good reason. He is an executioner, an electric executioner, well almost, since here he is, unemployed, once more, lack of clients, the State of Pennsylvania just having opted for lethal injection. Out of work, Howard returns to his first love, the wearying worship of Harry Houdini—our man, following Gary Gilmore's lead, is persuaded he is the unlikely grandson of the infamous magician. This belief, like digestion complicated by drowsiness, is the cause of surprising mental ferment. Thus, Howard has long believed that his ghostly granny is none other than Charmian London, Jack London's wife with whom Houdini fooled around, but thanks to more or less orthodox research he has come to wonder if his grandmother isn't instead the enigmatic ***SZUSZU***, the Electric Girl who shared the billing with Jumbo and the Human Cannonball. He'll have to talk about it with his mother, Emily, next time he brings her cookies at the hospice. In the meantime, he lets his cigarette fall into the circle of coffee that forms a mirror at the bottom of his mug, throws a glance out the window at the neighbor's garden, the dog sleeping in front of its kennel, its skeleton well protected under his fleabitten hide, a cat crossing the alley as if passing beneath barbed wire. Howard almost didn't sleep at all last night..

After having carefully avoided his wife Bess at the door of the kitchen and in the area around the living room, a Bess who does her best to limp to remind her husband that a pair of new shoes wouldn't be too rash a tribute, Howard shuts himself first in his study, upstairs.

The room offers the dust all sorts of runways on which various transitory objects leave their outlines from one day to the next (example: the imprint of scissors biting into the circumference of a quarter). A grimy PC occupies the center of the worktable and hardly whimpers when worried. At first the computer screen throws back at him an etching of a blurred outline, his own, and he must increase the brightness to the maximum for this muddy reflection to be followed by the block of instructions that he hasn't stopped embellishing for the last three weeks: **THE DESIGN OF AN ELECTROCUTION SYSTEM INVOLVES THE CONSIDERATION OF A FEW, BUT VERY SIGNIFICANT, REQUIREMENTS. VOLTAGE, CURRENT, CONNECTIONS, DURATION AND NUMBER OF CURRENT APPLICATIONS (JOLTS).** His fingers tiptap a few buttons while his eyes ascend slowly toward the photo of a girl in a swimsuit, subtitled ***SZUSZU* THE ELECTRIC BITCH** (1887-1909), and dedicated in soft pencil to Harry Houdini—***SZUSZU*** who seems to contemplate him from behind a windowpane frosted by boredom, her two arms raised in a flared V, each of her ten fingers connected by tingling cobwebs (30 volts certainly) to two generators trademarked **Godhison Inc.** Under the stiff swimsuit, breasts and pubis thrust out, even the seal of her navel, a tiny switch. In the background, a little to the left, one makes out the smudged silhouette of a sidekick decked out in a baboon mask: Houdini?

The screen of the computer excretes onto its surface a livid pool which knots into a loop before rushing to the upper right corner of the monitor. Without realizing it, Howard has turned the machine off. Without realizing it, he sat up straight and brought his big nose close to the glazed face of ***SZUSZU***, his tongue came out between his teeth, while below, against the frame of the monitor, the fabric of his pants strains against the contained arc of his erection. The lips of the woman seem to move away from one another, a hesitant mollusk parting and saliva forming a bubble, a—

Hooooward!

Too bad.

Bess is calling him.

She must have found, hidden under a corner of carpet, the magazine that Sam Turnpike handed over to him the other night at the *Bright Angel Bar* in exchange for a mega-round of drinks. Sam is his only friend, even if the only thing that interests Sam is setting Howard onto dubious paths, fornication for three or four, with fleeting women upon whom he experiments with all sorts of gadgets, you got no idea, since you haven't tried one you can't imagine. Vaguely disgusted, Howard ended up giving in, and he promised Sam to come join one of these pathetic orgies some evening, all the more reason to since his electric talents, he has been made to understand, were not without use. In the meantime, Howard looks in Sam's magazine for clues, for grounds for abandonment: those shaved and spreading slits, shiny gaping asses, breasts tightened on glans, pushed-in objects, too long hands, smiles daubed red, and, above all, those eyes which, mysteriously, don't follow you when the magazine slides left or right according to whether the right knee or the left knee hiccoughs while he yes beats yes off yes, all those attributes crammed between the glossy covers of the magazine must—imperatively!—be envisioned only from a servo-mechanical angle, yes yes yes, these are tools in a toolbox, nuts, screws, nails and rivets, greased pistons, and by supposing that the body is properly speaking this machinery which society covets, by supposing that by lubricating/plugging in/inserting one always ends up obtaining less rebellious surfaces, softer angles, and more subtle articulations, so there is most likely material there to invent something else, and since Howard Hordinary has no other desire on this earth than the worship of evasion and the improvement of a certain electrical device (which is waiting for him, on the mezzanine, where he will go soon, very soon), since he refuses Bess even the slightest soothing touch, why ever not, why not, not, make, here, there, ha-uh, a few, uh, adjustments, like like that, without a level, ah, or a chalk-line, oh, de-li-ca-te-ly, guesswork of the fle-uh-sh, yes, in the wood's knot the iron-hard fiber, **MARVELOUS**, see how the girl in the centerfold resembles can be mistaken misshapen misread for ***SZUSZU***, with a felt pen he closes her eyelids and puts his giant's index finger on her dwarf pubis, but of course nothing happens, flop-flop, the ink eventually stains the whorls of his flesh, and when he brings the finger to his tongue the taste he reaps isn't worth, far from it, a glass of bourbon even cut with water he cuts the current.

It isn't the magazine Bess has exhumed, but one more bill: electric components, soldering lamp, circuit breaker casing, three-phase wiring . . . *shit!* Howard sends back to limbo the portrait of his grandmother-hetaera and leaves his study. He passes past Bess without even favoring her with an ox-like wink and, body upset & mind warped, grabs his cluster of keys and goes down to the mezzanine, where nearly eleven years of sedimented illusions are going moldy: posters lit up in abbatoir red, boxes full of cards, scaled rings, dried bouquets, Gordian knots, volumes tattoed with gilded riddles—the name of Houdini repeated in all manner of publicity and bluff, extolled at the head of all the leaflets—all the flashy rubbish of the great Houdini, peritonized some seventy years earlier: ropes, chains, and, above all, handcuffs—The Maltby Dead Lock Shackles, The Extraordinary Bean Giant Handcuffs, The Regulation Double Lock Tower Leg-Irons, The Double Lock Tower Ratchet, The Navy Handcuff Slave Iron, The Nova Scotia Leg-Iron, & The Parish

Thumb-Screws & The Pinkerton Handcuff—

Enough!

Enough!

ENOUGH!

Have you ever seen a streetlayer collecting loose stone? Or consumptive phlegm? Or knacker carcasses? Even the worst profligate doesn't preserve in his mental tank all the asses he's penetrated. This mezzanine is a storeroom, a bazaar, an abyss—hullaba, sabbath, pitch—yeeuck—it's the winter of memories, the ice you must break by striking it with your heel before emptying your sluggish bowels. One door, then five steps to the worn lip, then another door, three point ten meters of hallway, a floor of packed dirt where Bud bottlecaps and cockroaches crunch underfoot, here and there the dull splendor of a quarter, congealed spit.

Howard only ever goes through here reluctantly, his backside kicked by remorse or domestic fear, his glands dessicated by the obvious fact of his own disaster.

In this pit, the outside world reaches him in irritating and muted frequencies, randomly piercing the walls of the mezzanine with the thin ice-axe of rumor. The light reeling through the solitary wiregrilled window barely dirties, with its uneven and floating lozenges, the grate which occupies the place of honor at the foot of the wall. Sometimes, rain collects in the garden's gravel and finds a path between the old joints, then dark, persistent, drips in. So the brick sweats, sparkles, slugs colonize it then wither with the return of the sun, then fall, raw snot.

A smell of torn up grass lingers as well.

Once more, therefore, Howard Hordinary has decided to come sound out/inhale/lick the raw fabric and the tepid leather of his straitjackets, quite inclined to don the toughest, even if that means struggling for a solid hour—arms crossed into an **X**, thorax compressed by the trussing strap with metallic buckles, all struggle reduced to its barest expression. The stakes are the following: to break up gesticulation to the extreme until it is no more than the imperceptible contortions of a demoniac and nearly invisible maniac, little gears of chaos. The day before yesterday, he met failure. Three hours to torque his body in the wrong direction, all his muscles rolled up, folded, refolded, and not a millimeter gained, not a nerve smoothed out, the feeling of being your own vise, of having padlocked skin. Forced to tear the canvas of the straitjacket on the rusty arc of an old spade, Howard was weeping about being so inept at so many things that he very nearly contracted tetanus.

Down here, the pink mortar peels and turns to powder between the bricks, piled up papers give off a scent of carrion dulled with straw. Howard presses the pear hanging above a turret of tires, and suddenly the luminescent bulb stamped with the initials of Godhison Electric Co., the Memorial Lightbulb presented by Edison to the Great Houdini for services rendered to the electric chair (and for which Howard paid three hundred dollars in an online auction, a first-rate web swindle), suddenly this cherished relic with glints of mica EXPLODES in a shoddy noria

tink[1]

tink[2]

tink[3]

tink[4] exposing a fat, bent, & ringed filament, which starts to glow red, to swell, stretching stretching stretching until one of its ends is freed from the brass spiral which forces it into a ring and turns toward him, toward HH, strangely snakish & complicit, staring at him with its bifid point from which pearls—pliip!—a spark which seems made of mercury or of stigmatic blood and which grazes, in mid-fall, his upper lip

—an ounce of volt, no more no less, that's enough. Howard lets out a gasp the size of a lump of phlegm, which he swallows again immediately, failing to choke

(and what happens belongs to something else, to another life, to another episode, the child's bottom lets loose a grown up shit which an old man's hand wipes away, the milk of life sours, bile rises, the body capsizes, one doesn't dare say when or how, everyone knows that, everyone has lived it and will live it, again and again.)

Here he is hostage to an obscurity of tightly-wound fibers of suspicious density, a shroud at once dense and dripping, ignorant darkness—sabbath, hullaba, pitch—muscular water. These are the new coordinates within sight of a less restricting space, a space from here on out built by the hands, widened by the feet, shaped by the head, a made-to-measure space which sticks to the body while anticipating its most minute movements, its most muffled contractions; another body, perhaps, veered away from itself, toward other enslaved flesh. A body in recovery or expansion, of varying dimensions, a loop of skin without beginning or end.

So Howard understands that his existence is nothing but diminutions, levitations, undulations, excuses, ether, forgettings, chains, nails, drunk shame, slow exertion, rust, abcess & absences, is nothing but the heart of a white irrationality so urine-stained that he can no longer distinguish it from the white of a still paler irrationality bearing a name [here that of the envied master forbearer = Houdini] and a mark [here his own = HH], because where does he think he comes from? from what god? from none! from a slit?zmoistened? distended by the growing pressure of a cracked and stubborn ram's cock? Blah. Howard knows quite well that the life of an escape artist is composed exclusively of disappearances, contractions, expulsions, moods and conspiracies, legendary suffocations, and thus thus thus why not act in his turn as Houdini, why not escape into the flesh of the illustrious magician and don all his wounds, all his memories, the Holy Lightbulb is broken, the seal-fastener deflowered, click-zarp—and after his flight from

Hungary, when his Rabbi father, having taken as his second wife Cecilia Steiner, transfused the name to him and his brothers in Wisconsin, in America, in the month of September 1876—barely landed, he received a new date of birth in exchange for the old, much too budapestiferous one, his name itself slowly rotted from the inside and he who was called Ehrich Weiss, the little prince of ether, through one of those phonetic trickeries which fall under the most atrocious patch jobs, became out of guttural shame—Ha—Har—Harry—Harry Houdini!

dismemberment of disgrace

The child Houdini spent hours staring at the coppered wounds of locks until retinal exhaustion imprinted their contour, the round top and crenellated sides, on the dark chamber of his eyeballs, then, later, after dinner and the inept goodbyes his mother thought herself obliged to bestow—*sleep well Ehrich and come back to us soon*—in the cave of his sheets, nervous fingers on his master skeleton key, he sculpted imaginary and malleable steel in every respect similar to this key—then, overcome by a drowsiness of geometrical inspiration, suffering from a *slowness* for which he didn't know any natural or biological counterbalance, he let the skillful and freshly opened instrument penetrate the hatched abyss which already was widening and trembling at its edges; hope was changed into expectation, expectation into drowsiness, and drowsiness into something else.

Later, on a plane that one could qualify as mental if it weren't by this point caked with blood, Houdini riddled his skin with cutely magnetized needles, twisted his body so as to bend it to the dictates of water in quintiple-thick coffins, dragged up from the cellar of his stomach a chain of razor blades soberly threaded on a strand of blue silk, a thousand deadly pennants still all sticky with bile, jumped shackled off bridges, was suspended from crane winches over the blind crowds of Mister Ford. He shut himself up, chained himself, buried himself, immured himself, suffocated himself, but each time pulled through, came through: maniac be praised!

But before gathering pins with his eyelashes at age nine, head down in an octagonal arena speckled with sawdust, feet harnessed to a pulley whose every creak seemed to warble his name, ehr-ich-weissss-ehr-ich-weissss-ehr-ich-weissss, before picking up needles with his teeth on behalf of the great Huber at age nine, Houdini had lost his magical virginity by witnessing the famous trick of the severed body, the Illustrious Trick of the Dismembered Body.

(Let's assume that all torture has, besides its share of absurdity, its portion of glory. Let's suppose that this glory, as colorful as it is, is not beyond titillating the glands, which, with an individual inclined to perpetual escape, become inflamed the moment a false miracle takes place. Let's agree on the fact that these presumptions and suppositions are the abstract equivalents of a hairshirt or of a dildo, and then it's better understood why young Harry, confronted with these barbarous playlets, felt that one woman would not quench his delight.)

Well. What happened? That evening (this must have been around 1882-1883), the illustrious Hyman gave his first performance in the city of Appleton, Wisconsin. He had spent three quarters of his existence wandering from villages to towns, from precarious exile to back alleys. Only his fluency of speech and his dexterity had saved him from a less exemplary fall. Tired of the tomfoolery of his friends the freaks, he had perfected a number assuring him renown & firewater, a number he imposed on his audiences with the presumptuousness of a meager despot.

After each performance, he washed his hands and made off for the brothel where, always, he found a girl sufficiently toughened to endure his ithyphallic sleight of hand. Hyman was a charlatan even when it came to penetration, and what he conjured away nine times out of ten prevailed over what he tried hard to make reappear. So, a good client. Five minutes on stage, sweating and haranguing, then schioup! applaud ladies and gentleman, the girl hardly needs to linger at the bidet.

ANOTHER MAN CUT UP TONIGHT

❀ ❀ ❀ ❀

A PROMISE! You were going to see what you were going to see, not one bit more, but jostle a little, all the same. Conjugal fervor would perhaps find matter for renewal. And then it wasn't expensive, a few cents, that would make a change from the designated local Quaker.

That evening, Houdini was the cut$^{u}_{p}$ man, the little allegedly chloroformed mannikin who men cowled in black sectioned with the consummate knowledge of artisan-butchers, using knives broad as palms and long as the arms of priests pointing out the sacrificial victim, which he was not, not yet.

And yet, the child didn't rise from the bench on which he sat, he didn't move to the front or pull himself onto the stage—he could have done it yes, he could have, if his fingers hadn't been hooked into the plumpness of his thighs, if his feet hadn't been shod with a lead as heavy as the torpor which ascends the roots then the trunk of a tree spared from lightning—no, this inept thing that he was then, and which was called Ehrich, and which was also named Weiss (this scion of the wife of an exiled rabbi whose placental sheath ended up under the fingernails of Hungarian skirmishers), this 1.05 meter high clod who sincerely believed that **AMERICA** was the name of a queen of Europe whose heartbroken beheaders had given to the vast continental whim where his mother had given birth (to him) for the second time since he was offered two birthdays, two enemy slopes for just one birth, a 24th of March 1874 at Budapest + a 6th of April also 1874 at Appleton, Wisconsin, so twelve days to be unborn and reborn & to cross the Atlantic impossibility, twelve days during which the baby discovered, at the mercy of swells and lulls, that to inflate his lungs was to block his windpipe all the more and to turn purple so as to better uterinize backwards and then expel oneself onto terra nova—no, that simpleton that he still was didn't dare lend himself to the accommodating magic of Dr. Hyman. All he experienced was by way of that depressing proxyhood which serves as courage for the impotent.

Because Harry had been subject to dismemberment for a long time, it had become a second nature and stopped him from enjoying that illusory coagulation of the senses that adults call identity. He was what? Hungarian? What did it matter, he had been demagyarized, wisconsinized late in the day, appletonized *on second thought*, as if with regret, indicted with remorse; they had already deboned him in more ways than one, his tiny body of three pounds 19 oz. having known exile and intra-uterine deportation. He knew only too well the torture of a thousand wounds, which since his birth the Chinese of his nightmares had inflicted upon him when, pilloried in a place as filthy as it was immense, inflamed by shouts and grimaces, a thousand men and a thousand women cheered the slow disjointing of his person—it was a dream that he often had, and ceaselessly perfected without knowing, the blade opened in him careful hems which immediately bled crimson loops, they peeled him, spelled him, called him, it was his name that they flaked off, that they scaled, he was the fished fish—*the fish on the dock!*—and the hooked worm; by the strength of unsealed fleshstrips, of lidless eyelids, they instructed him in the unctuous peeling of his name, a name which had as echoes only flayings, now Eric Weiss then Ehrich Weiss then Ehrich Prach and again Erik Weiss. And when, at the cost of a silly transplant, he became years later that inaccessible magician known under the trademark Harry Houdini, he had once and a hundred times more to pass through all sorts of disfigurations, he was shackled, trampled, articulated, he was, became, embodied Hunyadi, the ball-less, legless athlete, Hugh Deeny, the blind swallower of rusty sabers who pulled out his teeth, one per night, before the beautiful golden graveled eyes of Tess, the drunkardess with fingers of bone, the merry deadbeat Harvey Holmes of Bostonian parties who, limping stammering and thingamajigging as one expected, caressed your palm and pulled from it flowers which immediately blossomed into slender feathers, the subsequent explosion of which brought about the langorous chiming of chandeliers, and finally, finally, that cretin Mourdini, who put electric sparking Christs at the end of your nails with a single screech of his copper baton on his zinc torso, in homage to Nicolas Tesla, the apostle of the discontinuous current, the sworn and forsworn enemy of Thomas Edison.

Houdini escaped all this jumble of moods, passing and repassing three hundred sixty five and a quarter times, not once more, through the insolent cadaver of little Ehrich Weiss so as to—on the edge of a career that he considered today as adulterated as the best contraband whiskey and as worn out as the worst whore in Milwaukee—move forward under banners that he had had to embroider with hooks and jabs, move forward until he no longer felt the weight of the planks under his feet nor the hornets of applause from behind the velvet of the curtain, always moving forward without cease and, through the magic of a sizzling fright, backing away, absenting himself without absolving himself too much, and starting over, coming back, doing again what he had never done, yes, doing well what can only be done badly and doing badly what shouldn't be done, donning iniquitous tunics, odious togas, and seeming, yes, seeming, entirely, cut up and reassembled a thousand times, in the screaming pool of the violet spotlight which pinned him to the scenery and haloed him with a slightly silly gloom, and paying himself off with names crowned like monstrous molars, treating himself to a thousand epithets & other prestidigious titles, *by himself and others baptized*—**THE HANDCUFF KING!! THE UNDISPUTED KING OF HANDCUFFS!! THE WILD MAN!! THE GREAT ESCAPOLOGIST!! THE MONARCH OF LEG SHACKLES!! THE JAIL-BREAKER!! THE MASTER MONARCH OF MODERN MYSTERIES!! THE MYSTERIOUS HOUDINI!! THE KING OF CARDS!! THE MASTER OF MANACLES!! THE WORLD'S GREATEST MYSTIFIER!! THE WORLD-FAMOUS SELF-LIBERATOR!! THE HANDCUFF HOUDINI!!**

THE SUPREME RULE OF MYSTERY!! THE MASTER MYSTIFIER!! THE GREATEST NECROMANCER OF THE AGE!! THE GREATEST ENTERTAINER OF THE AGE!! THE JUSTLY CELEBRATED ELUSIVE AMERICAN!! THE MAN WHO WALKED THROUGH WALLS!! THE MASTER OF ESCAPE!! THE WONDER WORKER!! THE MANACLE MANIPULATOR!!—then, in front of the cameras, rigged up still and always, and faithful to the gemellary guillotine of his initials, idiotically naming himself systematically and successively: Harvey Handford!!! Howard Hillary!!!!! Heath Haldane!!!!!!

Hashamed Human, he didn't dare use, and yet he was one.

That's how, before gathering pins with his eyelashes at age nine, head down, feet harnessed to a pulley whose every creak, in the sinister octagonal arena speckled with sawdust, seemed to warble his name, *ehr-ich-weissss-ehr-ich weissss-ehr-ich-weissss-nicht*, before picking up pins with his teeth at age nine on behalf of Huber, he had lost his magical virginity by witnessing *the famous trick of the severed body,* The Illustrious Trick of the Dismembered Body, carried out by The Fabulous Hyman, a trick in which your body is split, as if the only temptation was to offer you a bitter anatomy lesson before the very eyes of your fellow man, while, while, while, quite obviously, no one, but no one, in this place, from the highest tier to the dampest wings, had, to that day, imagined that a body divided could constitute an original attraction, so many cadavers had they all seen and lifted and buried and mourned and cursed and even sometimes dug up so as to better forget them.

Dr. Hyman died the day following this final performance, without knowing a kind of warped vocation had just been born within the public he was swindling.

Midnight had passed when the old magician let his daily bottle of whiskey roll under the bed of a woman named Francesca. Fly done up, he was already snoring when the sound of breaking glass made him roll over in his completely sperm-spun sleep. Outside, a storm broke branches and gusted against the shutters. Rain poured down in buckets. Banging everywhere, at the door, in the eardrums, in the sky. And in Hyman's dream: something which wasn't working, something which was creeping and clucking, badly mended memories which were a bit awkward, a voice as well, raucous and witty, which spoke to him, incited him, provoked him; he got up or thought about getting up. Francesca stood at the foot of the bed, breasts still possessing the signature of his dirty nails, she held in her hand a candle with a diameter so large and a fuselage so unusual that he believed the dream was lasting forever; a flash of lightning seemed to dissolve behind the window and discharge itself from the tip of this extraordinary candle, there was a small little click and suddenly the guts of Hyman the charlatan were tired of chatting under his paunch, his glottis blocked itself with a dry stroke, *clok!*, his spine snapped out like a driving belt farting bastard too late bastard too late too late for good old Hyman. Francesca pleaded justifiable dementia to her lover the sheriff.

A year later, Harry had another revelation. It was in 1884, he was ten years old, a circus had just set its big top in his city. Before his eyes a magician made aces spring up at the ends of his fingers, freed rings which resembled those his mother hid under her dress, then droned out solved equations like rabbit droppings.

Samuel R. Lynn, also called The Great Merlynn.

Ladies and gentlemen I ask you for the greatest attentiveness and the modest price of your naïveté eight pence thank you.

Zim-boom

In the first row the kids pinched each other and rubbed their knees against the wood of the platform. Jack Hoeffler, the local wino, threw his head back and let loose a yee-haw thick with hacked up snot. The silence matured bit by bit out of giggles and the scraping of chairs. Outside a dog barked. The Incredible Merlynn pulled up his sleeves, revealing laudanum-swollen forearms, and let his eyelids construct an inspired look. He cast an eye to the right toward the young girl of thirteen who, in tights and swimsuit, moved from one foot to the other as if to tamp down a platform that was threatening to warp.

Profiting from the shift of public attention to the girl's thighs, Merlynn gave a shake to his left cuff, a shake which, reverberating in imperceptible waves along his tensed muscles, dislodged some mechanism situated upstream from his elbow. At the other end of the stage, a clock struck twice, ding, making all the gazes swivel, dong. The diversion lasted only a sliver of a slowly spinning second. From the hands of the great Merlynn spurted eleven red roses, where a moment before only a little black velvet had frothed.

The child who Harry was then demanded from his memory the exact architecture of these tangled gestures; he tried to restore the chronology disrupted by the girl in the green swimsuit, forcing himself mentally to augment the contrast between the black of the impression of the sleeve and the white of the silences. But a coarse power held it back, he was just stirring up muddy faces, didn't succeed in shaking up the cripple coughing with impatience behind him. *Scheisse*, he whispered, I'm going about it wrong. But when Merlynn performed the next act, that of the Severed Body, Harry tensed all that he had to tense and didn't miss a bit: he folded the girl into her swimsuit, the swimsuit into the scenery, transformed the clock into stone and hammered the two nails of his eyes into the hands of the magician. Then time cracked very tenderly and its lines became points, its angles curves. Inverted by the lens of his tension, a sort of anatomical cutaway danced for him the chaconne of illusion. He saw the black bottom sway its hips, the mutilation table roll millimeter by millimeter, the false limbs slide onto the numb arms of the fettered victim, he heard the rubbing of felt on fabric, the rolling of joints within the flesh of the elbows and the phalanges, heard the elastic snap under the sleeve and the wire vibrate against the wrist—but, of course, he no longer saw the surprise, the miracle, no longer felt terror, even disguised. So he waited for the third act, that of the saber, to compel his vision into a rhythm at once slower and less cadaverous. The cutaway Lynn had briefly been metamorphosed into a carefully made-up automaton, warped in a subtle outfit, working in jerks and glides. Harry/Ehrich let the ding and the dong of the clock reverberate so that the stage again became a vibrating eardrum, and translated each of the words supposed to divert attention from the cover up into musical notes, without deforming the impact which he had with great pains opened up. Which made Lynn seem more like his father deboning a fowl or punishing his older brother. At the same time, there occurred a curious compression in his bowels, a bubble popped, blood which he didn't recognize streaked an organ which he was completely ignorant of, or nearly so, the surface of his skin cracked, the nape of his neck tensed. Having approached him without anyone else's knowledge, the girl in the green swimsuit released her name into the well of his ear: ***SZUSZU***. A name which fell straitly and firmly into his ear without brushing against its walls, a pebble perfectly shaping around him the tube of silence until a pedestal rises up within him from out of nowhere and lets itself be marked with a seal—underwear soaked, he went back home, understanding that a magician's life was composed of noises and leakages, of minute obscenities concealed in the folds of his palm, of keys, terrors, kept hungers. A lesson that would have to be transformed into a destiny, at the very least.

Henceforward, the girl in the green swimsuit didn't stop expanding under his sheets like vegetative evidence that needed to be constantly watered by tears and other spurts. She became the fluid of illusion itself, the necessary impetus for the brutal metamorphoses, the spring-latch holding down the trapdoor of surprise, the prestidigital beyond of his destiny, his discontinuous cum generator. Beginning the next day, he paced the streets of Appleton searching for her shadow. But Lynn had struck camp, leaving as the only vestiges the sawdust of his stuffed wildcats and the grass trampled by Unthan, the Armless Wonder, the ogre with neither arms nor bad temper who played the violin with his feet, flooding the audience with the funereal strains of *Asleep in the Deep*, that freaks' hymn which recounts the mortal agony of a sword swallower abandoned by a snake woman, and swallow he will, thousands of knives, alone in his hive, like a bee that swirls, for she left him in a swoon, leaving him not a single spoon, *and with him we all weep, asleep in the deep, asleep in the deep . . .*

Edison had just come onstage and sparks were flying in the wings. Besides, one no longer called him Thomas Edison, but the Illustrious Godhison, the wizard of Menlo Park. *Lux et voluptas*, it was time to choose . . . Five years it lasted, five years in which they hired and fired, groped in the dark and gave up without for an instant stopping the wild importation of always more costly materials, under the nose of customs and before the very eyes of the Attorney General, copper from Zambezia and platinum from Columbia, whole railroad cars of spools, of filaments. Armies of glassblowers running relay from five in the morning to eleven at night spluttering into long tubes that immediately metamorphosed into shining balloons; dozens of reformed gangsters were charged with ensuring the security of Godhison and his premises. Because here security was essentially virginity: the competitors were rabid and to drown them you first needed to stop them from getting friendly with Factory secrets. Indeed no day, no night, went by without a stranger being caught hastily copying out lines which, very often it must be said, were only a jumble of obscenities, put down hastily by an engineer furious from having thought himself denied a raise. The punishment was always the same: one hour on the knees of the Dynamort, after which the intruder left with a light step, no longer sure what sex he was, what nationality was going to claim him, in which direction he should turn.

Between these walls set with barbed wire and sprinkled with crushed glass, workers and electrons exchanged insults, challenged each other, busted each other, while the current bent, bent, going until it bit the dust and chewed it up to regurgitate it ten, a hundred, a hundred and fifty meters farther, in the form of a blue and green burst which was systematically reflected in the eyes of the gathered engineers, piercing their irises so as to better imprint on them an articulated lightning gash, a sort of z-shaped fire escape—and later, when they returned home, drunk, this scar continued to blind them, to superimpose itself on all that flattered their retinas, as if the entire world, and in particular their room, its walls, the bed, were cracking, and that through this capricious fissure fled all their fatigue, and themselves along with it. It goes without saying that all this time Master Godhison continued to hurl abuse at them, confederating them with clouts on the head, ogling them, castigating intuition as soon as it took the form and the velocity of an obsession or shriveled up in the soundproofing of muteness, sermonizing and tripping up the dreamers, dismissing with one hand or with an equation all those who dared to alternate the current or cuddle up to the dynamo, but sometimes also complimenting, stroking, because he was Godhison, the great centipedic brain, the sulfur shit propelled by the pushbroom of profit, Godhison the Father *and* the Son, and many spirits still as if they had never suffered nor been dethroned, the stern Manitou, the archgolem in person flooded in pan-electric fonts to spread neither light nor terror, but humiliation in all its forms. The care that the old Godhison took in breaking surrounding backs commanded respect. Nobody dared remark to him that, sometimes, he collected errors as if they were funky florins, no, that would have been to risk one's wages and the seat of one's pants, much better to crawl and count, count in time.

The last day of trials had arrived, Godhison was supposed to deliver to Southwick & Co. that very evening the calibrated results of his research. The Death Commission was in fact awaiting his verdict before ratifying the Bill for the electric chair—in his Auburn prison cell, the prisoner William Kemmler didn't yet know how roasted he would be. That's why that morning Godhison pulled a lever and shouted: *Let there be light!* Zap! and everybody took it up the ass, from the infantile baboon all scabbed and faltering who was sucking beatifically on burnt out bulbs to Jeremy, the brachycephalic genius brought in by the engineer Kohler—zap and re-zap! the commotion started immediately in the immense hanger of the Godhison General Factory, a veritable cathedral of sheet metal and brick entirely consecrated to the Wicked Voltaic Witch, hard-won rectum of a certain America, repository of antibodies and anti-trusts, parody of a system with coarse prostheses and iridescent appendixes, where men the equivalent of badly bungled nerve bundles stamped around, struck one another, barking out a round of orders and formulas, half-opening their valves only at regulated intervals, pissing in an iron pot or shitting in a smelting bucket, where men fueled on the worst wells of servitude pared back avidly and with delectation their domestic life, their emotions, their nightmares.

Overwhelmed by an attack of acute obsequiousness, the engineers finally presented Godhison first with a dog answering to the name of Joshua, an unlikely mastiff with brown fur, which their boss immediately wedged between two electrodes before sliding beneath its belly a zinc basin all a-lap with a green and steaming liquid. The animal yelped. An engineer shaved its ears. Another made an incision in its rear leg so as to slide in a metal rod off of which projected a bunch of red and blue wires. Godhison smiled, and slowly lowered his head until his chin touched the third button of his black vest. At this signal, chief engineer Kohler hurried over to operate a cogwheel which emitted a coppery sigh before turning over on itself. The tangle of neon covering the ceiling of the warehouse seemed to go breathless, and drifts of shadow took advantage of this to copulate between the joists. The dog shat. An unbearable phosphorescence developed around its hindquarters, roasting its fur and breaking its spine.

Godhison took notes, under the cataleptic stares of Brown and Southwick, his future honorary executioners, come to watch the preliminary deflowerings. A few steps away, in a glass cage that was monkey-wrench-proof, strike-breaker-proof and reporter-flashbulb-proof, Dr. Bodie's Dynamort clucked like a crazed chicken.

The trussed up mutt extended its paws as if a sledgehammer had crashed into it at mid-spine, the flaps of its chops stood out, a crude sound shook it then it sat back on its back paws, sat up and begged as if its immanent death were a lump of sugar disguised as the sun, then pirouetted on itself one last time and literally exploded.

So they presented Godhison with a baboon, a hateful bastard who tore all that it touched to shreds. Godhison paralyzed its two forearms with a voltaic spatula then cauterized its lips and sewed shut its eyelids. When the current came, the creature quavered out its scales, which tore from the engineers farts of saintly surprise. It didn't go all that well, and the Godhison Factory had begun to smell like a small mass grave.

Kohler gave signs of swooning and wiped his forehead with sheets of equations. Above him, the hands of the large pneumatic clock hadn't finished redistributing helpings of bitter delay: more than an hour, still three-quarters, soon 42 minutes . . .

Overcome with panic, they offered him a mule, then a walrus, then a lamb, and to end with a baby elephant.

The mule lasted eight minutes. The walrus seven. The lamb caused a short-circuit and was transferred to the kitchens. The baby elephant, strangely enough, ejaculated.

All in a day's work, concluded Godhison, arranging his pencils.

with the assent of the whore-earth

Dazed by the inertia of the flesh as we all are whenever it comes to structural change, Howard cuts a path into the mezzanine with his hips and elbows, finds the crate that his ex-mentor Alfred Leuchter sent him a few weeks earlier, pulls free the top, *schkrumph*, forces the nails to spurt out of their rusty holes, *srup srup srup*.

Immediately smells assault him that his body recognizes and gathers up, like a crab does its soft-bodied offspring.

First, he savors the gray and dense effluvium of things dead, like a tenuous sound followed by a burning echo which goes off to scorch the muffled siphon of one's ear, then it's a bouquet of heated wood, of strained leather, of numb metal, of blind metal, which creeps into his nostrils and runs off to awaken several neuronal clusters, which, after having followed billions of differential loops in a hundredth of a second, give instructions to certain inferior nerve endings to contract the muscles of his scrotum, releasing in exchange a rather shameful memory which quite naturally combines the defecating function with sexual stupor.

Not unapprehensively, Howard strokes the cuffs intended for his wrists one after the other. Into the screen of sticky dust which covers the back of the chair, he traces with the spatula of his right thumb his own initials—HH—which he imprisons after reflection—or nostalgia—in an inverted heart, a fleshy drop calling to mind the oblong ass of his magnetic whore ***SZUSZU***.

The examination continues, somewhere between stupor and clumsiness. The forward hoop is still deformed by the thousands of beads of sweat that it has soaked up. Howard's lips travel up and down it like the bulging of an eyelid. Its taste is bitter, but it speaks the same language as he.

In the half-light, his right forefinger locates the polished ivory switch, strokes it, then honors it with the pressure of his flesh. A modulated buzzing makes itself heard somewhere behind the chair and an orangey glimmer sizzles between the fibers of the wood.

On their own, the soles of his shoes find purchase on the whore-earth and stamp out two-phased waves which go swelling and pirouetting outward. Howard's gaze lands on the panel, within which jumps, lying at the extreme left of the dial, the needle of the voltimeter. The numbers form a third of the arc in which each zero 0pens a h0le in s0mething b0t wh0t?

The footrest has been planed, sanded, soaped, chlorinated, so as to neutralize the odor of feces and urine released nonstop by those who, before him, have been seated there to fry & atone for their crimes. William Kemmler, Charles Bonier, Martin D. Loppy, William, Chester Gilette, Mary Farmer, Albert Wolter, Charles Becker, Sacco & Vanzetti, the whole troop of the great toasted—all his predecessors, seated smoking howling, along with their sweat, their fear, their giggles. Because before our man Hordinary, there was a great consumption of electrons, all of a devised pain, a thousand reformulated positions, before him, flesh wasn't known to be so electric and still lay in wait for burns, gushes, hypodermic vexations; it performed as meat and as butcher, thought itself animal, had of elasticity only its own cracked surface, of the organic only its hidden combustion. Nothing to permit it to pass through the twinned eyes of a plug and penetrate the kingdom of subjective particles, where Howard is going this evening.

He is only two fingers away—thumb + forefinger and, if needed, middle finger—from ***SZUSZU***, his Sweet Electric Whore (S.E.W.), his Tender Plug (TP™). He is going to establish a connection, and this time it will be very different from the dotcom cuddlings with virtual microwhores that his PC offers to him with each click of the mouse. Over, the crypto-neural repartee of the net! Howard has known for ages that computer screens, like pizzas and mirrors, have no backs, no thicknesses, absolutely nothing to offer to tooth or nail. Screens are windshields stained by droppings steaming out of still invisible orifices, you can't chat with these things, ten years from now they will make them from Lycron Kevlar™, you'll slide them into the frames of your glasses like so many lenses restless for germination and you won't think about them anymore; worse, you won't notice them anymore. But fingers in plugs, that's something different, isn't it, another speed, it's primitive electrotorture . . .

Feeling aroused by vertigo, Howard forestalls himself and turns around at the speed of his whipped blood, his buttocks tighten, his knees flex and crack, everything in him sits down, capitulates, moans, his forearms align themselves with the two oak arms, the nape of his neck searches out the rigid upright, his eyelids harden, his cock rises and moistens—a little.

There are then pricklings on the rounded surface of his fingernails where, the baseness of the tension demands it, the nerve filaments are jumbled according to a binary schema, active/reactive, then are tangled again, then break. The leather straps tighten on his wrists and his ankles, the head strap engraves mauve and livid parallel lines on his forehead, which will soon follow confused ideas and other ectoplasmic fly-specks extorted by the medium from the marrow—strand by strand his hairs isolate themselves, dismantling the conductive plait, standing up, at their tips are born glimmers of spectral essence, reflected in them is the small gray alpha of birth and the dark omega of the final tumble, his pupils dilate by fits and starts through seven spheres, seven cylinders inserted into one another: that of fascination (1) inserted into that of oblivion (2) inserted into that of illusion (3) inserted into that of escape (4) inserted into that of slow death (5) inserted into that of the greatest cold (6) inserted into that of—? *crilc-zerp.*

Howard doesn't know what the seventh circle is nor if it is true that it includes all the other circles—his brain in his cranium in the head-strap of the electric chair in the mezzanine of this house where he vegetates with his wife Lady Mad Beß who ptomaine poisoning has reduced to compulsive vomiting and to invective—or if it opens elsewhere, if it will open for him on the elsewhere, the beyond. He has the feeling of being curled up on the inside, messed with by moray eels, by singing canker sores, tickled by minute adipose whips, ruptures occur at all levels, fissures breeding other fissures, coagulations of ideas fall heavily into flared tubes, images stuck to one another contort, strut about. This hits Howard sharply inside.

Ouch! His skin sweats oozes smokes, it produces fluids and humors, restores the filth accumulated in his pores, this filth that no other skin has been able to draw out, and especially not the starchy skin of Bess, the so-pure alcohol of fear imbibed evening after evening and which for ten years has formed a muffled layer within him. Muscles arch in him which until then didn't exist and which curiously smell like beef, father, revolt, muscles similar to greasy levers, destined for no other task than to open up the body to itself.

These are the things that he knows, that he has gone through, islets of intensity that he more or less visited a long time ago, when at the exit from adolescence he found his body submissive to the fluctuations of the sexual marketplace, each feature of his anatomy rated and deducted, passed between the fingers of languid solicitresses. Howard thought then that the discharge that extinguished his fantasies emanated from the subtle core of his being, thought that the terminal of desire and the terminal of pleasure were connected by a current born in the interstices of his personality. But he discovered little by little that the rhythm of these urges was orchestrated by something other than a so-called intimacy, that the cacophony of panting and dashing about had as its great controller the thousand and one artifacts of the society in which he developed. Now, when he got a hard-on, he knew that it wasn't because of such and such hairdo or cleavage, but rather because of the moisturizing cream applied to the neck of his partner, the same cream that you saw on every street corner, on five by three meter billboards, and whose fragrance was subtly distilled in the ink which was used to print newspapers, which were used to imprint his olfactory memory, which was finally used for something. It wasn't the distinctive ass of Dinah or Jenny that he coveted, but the inverted double globe which she engraved, dented, into the seat of his Buick whose name was always being sung on the radio; the arm which excited him so much would reappear everywhere, extended toward the most visible object in some grocery store, or else put over the shoulder of a bank advisor who smiled at you on television with his sweet pedophile's smile, or else concealed in a perfect cast on which insurers were going to scribble cryptic clauses. The teeth of his conquests were no longer the subtle instruments of biting but the spokespeople for a chemical whitener concocted somewhere in a laboratory that didn't hesitate to recycle the carcasses of animals, animals whose fur was used to dress those models who turned on the pages of the magazines open on his knees while his pants settled around his ankles like a puddle, like a limestone deposit. By sheer force of consuming aggregates of labels and advertising statements, Howard lost control of his emotions, didn't manage to negotiate the curve of irresponsibility which was silhouetted on the horizon and found himself catapulted completely off the road into the scenery, scenery which he went through, pierced, tarnished. When the wheels stopped spinning under the empty sky, he pulled himself up out of the carcass of his body, crawled up onto the shoulder, and saw that the other spontaneous combustion vehicles were still rolling, ever more quickly, avoiding him gracefully with disgruntled flicks of the wheel.

After that, he had to search for a way to start up again all those things that stalled out at every moment of the day, to reinstate the slightest swerve as inoffensive sign language, and then speak, speak in a steady voice, without fits and starts, to recite the list of phrases which permitted the closing up of consciousness and slowed the dismantling of urges. It was a painful (because painless), cruel (because insensible) apprenticeship. Maturity slowly calcified him, he forgot the flora of his first frights, moved forward into the unbroken light of collective life. But a strange mechanism continued to hum within, a smuggler's microchip, and that's how he decided to devote his spare time to the construction of an ergonomically reliable detonator.

Now that he is seated, everything about him rises.

Thenceforth, the executioners hired by Godhison spoke, danced and jerked off with the Dynamort developed by their boss's assistant, Dr. Bodie—digesting to the rhythm of its voltaic pulsations, breathing its bronzed exhalations, dreaming of it when energy would desert them and throws them onto their palettes—they maintained with it what hostile engineers of the flesh would have thoughtlessly qualified as sexual connections, about which they would have been mistaken, since the pleasure that the electric executioners pulled from the vulvaed diodes of the Dynamort didn't appeal to any organ, didn't excite any even vaguely erogenous zone; if there was a shock—and indeed there was a shock—it was unquestionably peri-nuptial: the electric executioners didn't *penetrate* the body of their Dynamort but rather gave themselves up to unusual procrastinations, surprising silences and slow sidlings, gratifying her with strokes so fluently alternating that they themselves were passed through by it, not knowing until then that at the tip of their fingers, in the remarkable convolutions of an often calloused pad which, normally, took hardly any precautions with metallic things, circulated a loving knowledge, a predisposition for irradiating contacts. In short, a talent for microscopic erections (however it would be unfair to attribute to the electric executioners more tactile ignorance than they had—their electric baggage was far from being non-existent since all had already experienced, often several times, the grand sensation, yes, all, one day or another, had treated themselves to a quick trip to the land of surprise, furtive lovers of the touchy Sparky, be it in the form of an ambiguous embrace ((one hand pressed to the bulging surface of the generator, the other slid into their pants, thumb and index finger pinching at intervals of 4.5 ohms/second the bulbous skin of the scrotum, one foot on the platinum planchette, the other stuffed into the strange gutta-percha slipper they never failed to bring along)), be it in the course of more controlled and less risky experiments—thus Westinglord, long in the service of the Godhison Factory, had had the privilege of trying the first Electroblivion, a formidable and secret engine applied until then only to enraged baboons, the regulation of which sent into a trance the most mentally armoured of engineers).

Accomplices of the deadly spark, sole representatives to this day of the United States of Electric Execution, disparagers of the gallows or despisers of lethal injection, in love with electrons of ever-changing polarity, they were, according to their families and before they espoused this new vocation, bastard faggot stand-ins for first-rate sons of bitches, *fucking lazy sons of so many unfuckable bitches!* Dr. Bodie had recruited them by drawing on the files of hospitals, keeping only those who had been treated for partial and mild electrocution.

One of them was called Alfred West. This New York bricklayer had been struck by lightning in

June of 1880 while he was conversing with two friends (Matt and Boss) under a tree, at Fort Lee, in New Jersey. The thunder deafened him even before it made the windowpanes of the neighboring grocery store explode in a shower. Thrown more than six meters from the tree trunk, he recounted his brutal misadventure as follows: "It's a see-saw, you gnaw on your own guts, your hair starts talking, it squawks in your nerves, things stop around you, they break into sevenths, eighths, noises get tangled into one another, hundreds of doors shut themselves again all over your body then open, banging like shutters, a detail scratches your eye like a hooker's fingernail, there's nothing more than that, this detail, a bone lodged in the throat of your fucked brain, and then an emptied chest, a hoof kick which runs you through." Alfred West regained consciousness at the exact moment when he heard the doctor declare him dead. The lightning had caught his thorax, where he flaunted a five by three centimeter burn on the right side of his throat, and on his right leg, which still shivered as if ants were rushing through it. The jolt had also burnt off his right shoe. He found his watch eight meters from the tree, without hands but with the crystal intact. His two legs stayed numb more than three hours, after which he walked as if the ground was strewn with embers or dog turds. He had to stay in bed for three weeks. Dr. Bodie got in touch with him the day before he got out, and their interview revealed that Alfred West, far from being gun-shy, wanted only to relive this unique experience, which had opened his eyes "and many other things." He was the first recruit.

Others followed. Soon Godhison General Electric was operating non-stop. In spite of the failures, in spite of the accidents, in spite of that love for the short-circuit which seemed indissociable from the chair, tiny progress, like little technological breezes, ended up sufficiently swelling the silent, deadly electro-fart. And the machine was declared ready to roll. In neutral, but nevertheless ready to roll.

All that was missing was a volunteer. This was William Kemmler—also known by the name of Billy Hort—who was the first to raise his hand, not without having first brought it down, duly equipped with an axe, on his companion, Tillie Ziegler, and this 26 times in a row.

His sainted reduction to ashes took place August 6, 1890. The first jolt lasted seventeen seconds. "And there you have it," declared Southwick, "the pinnacle of ten years of travel and study. From this day on, we shall experience a higher degree of civilization." But one of the witnesses present remarked that Kemmler had cut his hand with his fingernail during the jolt and that blood was still dripping from the wound. The criminal wasn't totally fried. Blood trickled onto the armrests, saliva frothed in the corners of his mouth, his eyelids flickered, he regained consciousness. The Dynamort was again put into action while Southwick conferred with Dr. Bodie and the Godhison set combed over diagram after diagram. The second jolt caught the criminal right in the ass. Kemmler leaped in his straps, one of which tore clean through. A smell of grilled beef filled the room, smoke rose from the head of the condemned man, and a blue flame spurted from his spine. A trumpeting sound swelled his gag. The current was cut. The man collapsed into himself—poor conductor, poor loser, poor husband. His clothing was already undergoing slow but steady ignition.

In 1890 medicine assessed that a body had given up fighting as soon as it no longer gave off any heat. Kemmler's body remained incandescent for several hours, and the autopsies had to be delayed to keep the coroner from burning his fingers. But what was secretly hoped for was really and truly produced: the assassin had released, at the moment of death, a considerable amount of cum—*a large quantity of dead spermatozoa.* An army of little future killers had just perished in the underpants of this mad dog: at least there was always that.

Pain has him tenderly, violently by the balls like a silk-padded vise. His thumb bends and inscribes a purple half-moon into his palm, hands as invisible as they are robust spread his thighs. It's as if he found himself in the first row of a movie theater, facing a screen-flower, a screen-noria, haunted by images of war, bits of Vietnam of Kosovo of Iraq, nothing figurative, nothing which stinks of flag-waving, but instead sounds that have again become images, shouts changed into luminous motion, the opposite of an epic poem released in spirals onto his irises. It kills raps smashes salutes, it sings & giggles, it's backward epilepsy, a unique opportunity.

Howard Hordinary becomes the object of disturbing ectoplasmic changes, a stickiness which was skin comes unstuck from his face to form, a few centimeters from his own lips, a perfect oval, which is immediately lanced by a smile. It seems to him that he recognizes in this milky mask the clammy Miss ***SZUSZU*** Hurst, the epileptic siren with almond eyes, with titanium eyelids, with a bit too long nose which fear flares out superbly, with oily rust-red and blue hair, which he has never breathed in except in the framed photo above his computer, but intoxication is such that each and every time steel and lavender are blended in his memory—clrc crlc crlc—the face shrinks and, like a blister, explodes, giving way to a staticky night underscored with pounding blows: pum han pun han pum pum pum

somewhere an elephant collapses like a building of gray stones—rfrfrf-kllIii—a baboon tears out his electrodes, wheezing—crlc crlc—a cry bursts out, darkness spurts from everywhere, but Howard's penis grows flattens out becomes silver, atrociously sharpened, swallowed by a sticky larynx, and goes off to join up with various objects in the pit of his stomach.

(relieved he recognizes the famous act of the Swallower of Anything and Everything, *the great trick* of the human ostrich),

then emerges, making the little round bulbs, which all carry the seal of the **GODHISON FACTORY**, *chime.*

The ceiling of the mezzanine clouds over, its cracks disgorge a pink plaster, piles of shadow settle in the four corners of the room, the wood of the chair cools, the needle sweeps the red of the voltmeter with metronomical oscillation. The siren of a police car reaches him like the screech of a fingernail on the blackboard of his nerves.

His legs are starched with animal stupidity, see how he gulps like a fish—*like a fish on the dock.* The leather goes slack around his wrists and ankles.

It isn't enough, he thinks, I want more, i want more, I want ***SZUSZU***, and for

<<MAD Beß>>

to shut up, for frustration to knock her out and lock her into her siesta, and for ***SZUSZU*** to finally torpedo me, for her to spurt thunder and hail, and for me to be each—*shak!*—hailstone—and each—*shak!*—hole which this hail pocks in falling, I want more (+), not the motionless shrew (-) but the Vertical, the Amperious and Conductive ***SZUSZU***.

He convulsively carries out a few adjustments.

The armbands slowly compress his forearms, carving livid notches into them.

Howard concentrates and unites with the chair.

With his fingers he strikes the ersatz door of his birth and makes the bell of his identity chime—tonk!—who is he? whoz-hee whoz hee whozzzheeeeeeee? howard hordinary? hourdinary? hourdini? his name disjoints itself in its desire for shedding skins and surnames of parental aberration, the little muscle of repudiation wriggles between the nerves of submissiveness, whozhee? whozhee? with what red-hot iron must he brand his hide to escape from the Pen, from the life-that-one-lives, from this immeasurable soot which stops him from shining?

Suddenly, like Braille next to the skin, responses, strokes:

HH?

Harry?

Eric Weisz?

Ehrich Weiss?

Ehrich Prach?

Hunyadi?

Hugh Deeny?

Haudyni?

Nordini? Mourdini?

Hungharry?

Hoo-dee-nee?

Oudini?

Houdin?

The Handcuff King?

The King of Handcuffs?

Bahl Yahn The Wild Man of Mexico?

The Supreme Escapologist?

The Great Jail-Breaker?

The Master Monarch of Modern Mysteries?

The King of Cards?

The Master of Monacles?

The World's Greatest Mystifier?

The American Self-Liberator?

—or, more prosaically, Howard Hordinary, executer of the down and out, unemployed executioner, apprentice formed and deformed by Alfred Leuchter, switch-flicker for serial killers, annoyed magician mired in the cute cult of Houdini?

Torture and vanitas! it continues of course, by additions and increments, agonies and minuets, virile atonements and soft orisons, Harry here, Howard there, until the intermittent current is changed into convulsive grammar, and the question comes back, like a small ohm clinging to the hindquarters, who is he? who is he? who is he? *a kettle or a kilt? a killer of cult?* what ampere swells him down here? who then will Howard be if he ever survives this ritual, this rhythm?

The Great Houdini?

or

The Handcuff Houdini?

or

The Master Mystifier?

or

The Greatest Necromancer?

or

The Greatest Entertainer?

or

The Justly Celebrated Elusive American?

or

The Master of Escape?

or

The Wonder Worker?

or:

the trapeze artist?

Shattered, he starts to invoke the moist spirit of ***SZUSZU***, murmurs/coaxes/lulls: Come, sit down, here, on me, your feet on my feet and your thighs on my thighs, the back of my chest against the wall of your back, your forearms on the old wood of my arms, my mouth in your hair, finally, my last trick, my last number, the ultimate highlight of the Ha'penny museum, of the dime-museum, the one and only swallower of brown hair, the human ostrich, the suzerain of the freaks, the Mexican savage finally returned to his phosphorescent female . . .

A slight improvement around the joints. The tongue less dry, too. The beginning of a penial reflex. He's going to win, the Electric Chair will be his Electric Whore (EW), his Hypnagogic Vehicle (HV) his Anti-Bess (AB), thanks to it he is going to experience the highest degree of dissipation, going to break the waterproof sack in which his speech, dully handcuffed, is tired of wriggling in its salivary coating—

Sing Sing! Sing me a song! Sing Sing! Sing me a song Sing Sing Song

It's Bess. Bess who's ringing for him: tinktink tink^{tink} tink^{tink} tink^{tink}, as, every evening, the copper testicle irritates the tin pod, shaken by an old string which creeps up the wall of his office, scales the ceiling above the steps, penetrates three walls before edging its way toward the salon and following the vertebral column of the chimney back to the bedroom where Bess, his now bedridden wife, gives the atrocious tintinabullatory pulse—*Sing Sing! Sing me a song! Sing! Sing Sing!*—In other words: Howard *quick quick quick my whiskey,* because ever since Bess was hospitalized for ptomaine poisoning, her eroded arteries require embalming booze, firewater, and, what's more, very expensive. But he has no desire to run down to the drugstore to fill up the JB. None.

He turns a deaf ear. Better: he becomes a deaf ear, a padded eardrum which absorbs everything and no longer quivers. Shocks, vibrations, echoes sink into him and are lost. His blood muffles and drowns everything.

Having reached the banks of limbo, he recalls Leuchter's advice: if the skin is smoking, tighten the straps and crank it up. The needle of the voltimeter sinks into the red like a hypodermic promise.

twilight of the freaks

In 1910, Huber's ha'penny museum, his famous ***DIME-MUSEUM***, was folded upon itself and its attractions, its big ass of planks and plaster sprawled on foundations which reeked of limestone and draining sewage. Harsh noises escaped from it, fizzled fanfares that you would have believed sprang up in hives or in whorehouses catering to old tenors. A fritter seller kept watch a few feet from the entrance, pallid behind the smoke of his sizzling oil. The façade peeled under the wind.

In the poorly irrigated meanderings of the howardian brain, behind his scorched eyelids, Houdini had finally rediscovered the trail of the girl in the green swimsuit. He pushed open the door and moved forward into long corridors as tormented as an epileptic's entrails. A black curtain undulated somewhere in front of him. He slid a hand between its folds and squeezed into the velvet slit.

The army of freaks were abruptly dragged from the remnants of the night. The Skeleton Girl rushed toward him immediately, humming "*come come come,*" then tenderly fractured herself from within into a murmuring constellation of diaphanous bonelets; her skin tightened, she wound herself around his torso and handcuffed strands of her wrists to the stakes of her ankles before offering him the spectacle of the double minaret of her knees, as well as the triangle of her taut thighs and the arid diamond which she wanted him to—***crilc-zerp***—Anvil Max surged up from a sort of cat-flap with a roar and hurled himself toward Houdini, hardened fists on his wheeled cart equipped with handles, chest swelled out, head thrown slightly back, as if the absence of pelvis and legs reared up in him some hostile pride—Harry backed up, collided with a wall, no, not a wall, but Mister Wall, the Colossus of the Carpathians (Fritz Bergen, twenty-two years old), breaker of chains and torturer of iron rods, his gaze so empty that one could have lodged within it a century of renunciations, a deaf and tepid building that drove him back like a tardy billpayer—Harry rolypolied and landed six meters further away, at the feet of Manfrede, the Human Fountain, and of his acolyte Miss Edith Clifford, the lightbulb swallower, and while the first spat out a brown geyser of small beer or croaked out drowned frogs, his companion gulped down a supple rod equipped at one end with a fluorescent bulb which immediately lit up the palpitating straits of her throat before diffusing its horrible brightness within bone and flesh, but Harry didn't want to see the lightbulb suffuse yellowly the vaginal vault into which she wished to dip his wick, he refused to—boarding from the stern, the Monstress Victorina turned up, he felt against his shoulderblades her triple-nippled breasts, let out a cry, the unbelievable mouth with vertical lips slid a dagger's kiss along the nape of his neck, he pushed her away, ran, stumbled, and cleared without reflecting or genuflecting the Hoop of the Dead which gave way in a fatal blossoming of pasteboard and red seersucker.

He heard laughter, ran, turned left, another hall, another door.

The dressing room was deserted. Harry stayed a moment on the threshold, hardly knowing whether he should trust himself to the salacious waves the place was emitting and move forward, defeated, or if he needed on the contrary to jostle each pernicious atom with contemptuous blows and let his anger fill the last cubic millimeter of space. He noticed then his reflection in the mirror set with lightbulbs; the visiting cards jammed into the frame seemed to judge him with their bold embossed letters, a whole fan of names in tow inviting flattering demanding ***SZUSZU***. And among these cards, his, lost, ridiculous, like a jack of spades stifled by two red kings, his name printed as if swollen by the helium of vanitas, **H O U D I N I**, with as a timid caption these few words: *for Miss Szuszu my electric sprite.*

He felt the dressing room shutting itself on him again like a casket on a corpse. The fragrance he was smelling wasn't only that of ***SZUSZU***, it was also that of all the bodies come to besiege her, drably foliated layers in which still swarmed the thousand and one maggots of flattery.

His feet seemed to press against moist pockets still filled with compliments, promises, like craquelured globes of seaweed, the noise quickly became unbearable, hundreds of mingled accents, rancid intonations; he was only one card among others, a jack trampled by aces. He sat down where ***SZUSZU*** put her admirable ass and looked at himself in the mirror, as if it were possible to distinguish not the reflection of ***SZUSZU***—the tain was much too corroded to have absorbed it—but that of the suitor which he had become since having seen ***SZUSZU***.

Behind him, someone pushed open the door of the dressing room and the motor of someone's breathing completely shifted the stability of the silence.

Harry closed his eyes. It had to be her. She of course had received his letter. "My Electric Cherie . . . " A hand landed on his shoulder and Huber's voice whistled in his ears.

There you are, Harry. You finally came. You came looking for her, didn't you?

Yes, answered Harry. I came. For her. Give me the Chair and let's get it over with.

Howard only wants the Chair, and of the Chair, he only wants its soul, in the same way the copper-jacketed bullet only wants the soul of the gun, its greased and cool casing, its science—the Chair, the **CHAIR**, the **CHAIR**, he sleeps in it, spends the night in it, rests in it, it is his old knocked-up lady, the gums for his molar-body, the leather pod in which to slip his warped foot, he wants it highbacked and dark, in oak and iron, covered in felt, Howard wants a Chair identical to his body, clad in a silvery lace, a feminine lace with starving lacis, and for this Chair to be heavy, for its weighty insolence to be seen and felt—in the Chair finally he lives, feels the scolopendrae, feels the spiders, feels the bites, the stings, the burns, the blows and the bursts, the caresses of yes and the pinches of no, he feels the flora and fauna, the tear-soaked fabric and the sap-sullied flesh, the corrupt silk and the volatile thrill, he feels the laughter of the rust awakening the iron too long asleep, yes, on the Chair everything groans everything jolts nothing flees, the memory of the first peeled fruit, the ignorance of that lacerated ass, which never stops streaking with blood, on the Chair his little infant's body settles, reclusive, sprawled, steeped in unbearable mammary quiescence.

Undoubtedly, our man Hordinary is cross about his life, which he would have liked to be more spacious (it wasn't in the least), with long galleries pierced by sparkling prospects, immense spiral staircases meeting at the top of a platform surmounted by a conductive dome (lead and worked copper), a life riddled with hallways bound by axes, with several levels, scanned by infrared tracers, completely dedicated to the negation of what was, until now, the very matter of his, of his life: matter half inert, half dead, like how after too many beers drunk on a couch you sprawl, remote in hand, zap-a-zap, ear folded on the cushion which crushes a magazine, eyelid agitated by tics as if a little bit higher up some fucking puppeteer was having fun teasing the human carp; wily matter, also, since due to sessions on his ecstatic shitter Howard continued dishordinarying himself, displacing himself, houdinizing himself more each night, disappearing by jolts and discrepancies, losing in hearing & sight what he gained in sweat and reincarnations.

After five years of apprenticeship under Leuchter, the dethroned executioner, Howard found himself again back at the beginning, and even a little further back, in the red, in that place where credit had been killed long ago.

Rotten luck had accompanied the Hordinary couple, like those little jointed dogs whose heads nod miserably on the back windowshelves of cars and who seem to taunt us each time we look in the rearview mirror. Woof, woof, nothing behind, nothing up front. Howard and Beatrice had already moved to a new State three times in two years. And each time, the motive for exile was the same: a county judge shook his humanist bell, public opinion became indignant, preachy, then the penitentiary system gave up the electric chair and sent *ad patres cum lethalis* injectionis a given rapist or serial killer. Yet another day to mark with a black cross for Old Sparky! And once again unemployment for Howard, electric executioner for his State, or else another.

A little everywhere in the American territory gas chambers and lethal injection systems vied gallantly to dethrone—that's the right term!—the good old 2,000 volt chair. Mississippi had toppled and Florida had fluttered its files since Alan "Tiny" Davistook, still comfortably seated in a brand new chair, started, *post mortem,* to bleed like a badly stuck pig from the nose or the ears, it wasn't clear which, but this had made a bad impression, a dead man who bled, no, honestly, might as well live Tudor-style and decapitate those people. Howard found this ridiculous and irritating. After all, Davistook weighed more than 370 lbs and suffered from hypertension (not to mention arthritis), besides the bastard ran on aspirin and Motron; now those things make the blood fluid, don't they, they stop it from curdling reasonably in the vein's siphon, and when the jolt occurs, beurk, see how you piss red milk, it's like milking a carcass. Pharmaceutical blunder, that's all, but like a tablecloth stained with Château-Margot, the shirt of the condemned man had handled the nasal flow badly. Tabloids doubled their print runs, judges brandished their gavels.

Old Sparky, the fake Flickerette, was judged shaky and immediately put away in a museum for rednecks badly in need of sensations. Ten cents per mini-jolt: at that price, thought Howard, whores better recharge their vibrators.

But that isn't all.

Two years earlier, as Pedro Medina posed before the shutter of memory, three hirsute flames thirty centimeters high (a foot of fire!) had spurted from the top of his head—the fault of sponges insufficiently saturated with saline solution, fastened askew on his temples . . . no, really, the toaster fucked up. Promptly, the next on the list, a certain Thomas Provenzano, was granted a stay of execution and was already being promised the anaesthetizing caresses of crypto-cyanide. In certain states, they even sketched out plans for the return of the gallows, springs and levers guaranteed, and somewhere south of Albany a voice was even hauled out to speak highly of the guillotine. French Doctor, very good! Soon, the strappado would pass for a technological wonder. And the silken garrote would be sold in all 5th Avenue shop windows, with or without extenuating circumstances. Nevertheless, Howard had worked relentlessly these last years. Based in Pennsylvania since Christmas of '78, coached by Leuchter, he wasn't lacking clients, and he kept their names pinned on a big sheet of paper above his desk, sometimes with brief annotations on their behavior, the composition of their last meal, a remark they had made before the switch was pulled. He remembered the face, the voice, the gait of each. He even managed to question them in his sleep to ask them if, really, when the 2,000 volts went through their bodies, didn't it produce in them a certain revelation, nothing religious, no, but nevertheless, something savory enough so that, all at once, the feeling that life was a marvelous phenomenon and not a series of prodigious nuisances, was imposed on them, without arousing either surprise or regret, just as an obvious fact . . . John Spenkelinj, Robert Sullivan, Anthony Antone, Arthur Goode, James Adams, Carl Shriner, David Washington, Ernest Dobbert,

James Henry, Timothy Palmes, James Raulerson, Johnny Witt, Marvin Francios, Daniel Thomas, David Funchess, Ronald Straight, Beauford White, Willie Darden, Jeff Daugherty, Theodore Bundy, Aubrey Adams, Jesse Tafero, Anthony Bertolotti, James Hamblen, Raymond Clark, Roy Harich, Marion Francis, Nollie Lee Martin, Edward Kennedy, Robert Henderson, Larry Johnson, Michael Durocher, Roy Stewart, Bernard Bolander, Jerry White, Phillip Atkins, John E. Bush, John Mills, Pedro Medina, Gerald Stano, Leo Jones, Judias Beunoano, Daniel Remeta, Allen L. Davis, Terry M. Sims, Anthony Bryan, Bennie Demps . . .

But the names were too numerous, the sonorities too varied, it could have been a basketball team or an Alcoholics Anonymous meeting, Gulf War veterans or victims of an air-crash. The cruelty was extinguished with them, and, over their corpses lightened of all dignity and dental particularities, had grown again the sad three-piece suit of media amnesia. Howard Hordinary himself could have appeared on this tedious list, attached to one or two crafty crimes and an incompetent lawyer. **GUILTY OF SELF-ELECTROCUTION!** *His nerve cells testify!* **NEW TWIST IN THE HORDINARY CASE:** *experts assess that Double H's cortex was not responsible at the time of the jolt of electricity . . .*

In the kitchen, Bess polishes the counter while cursing, her ass vaguely vengeful, an energy to her elbow which would give the most committed onanist pause. The sponge comes and goes like a crazed puck on the stainproof surface, the dirty water spurts, and the window above the sink, behind which a dozen or so sparrows look for a stave among the power lines, ends up looking like a cheap watercolor. What are they going to live on, she splutters, if Howard refuses to move into lethal injection or auto mechanics. All their savings have been wiped out by his houdineries, each dollar one-clicked away via the web for auction bids swollen by bytes. Every day, the postman flings onto their steps a package which, barely ripped open, reveals, in no particular order: a t-shirt with the magician in effigy, his inset face subtitled with a silly **MASTER OF KINGS;** unstickable stamps that show the escape artist in a swimsuit on some parapet or other in some metropolis or other; tempered steel musical handcuffs; straightjackets eaten away by the salt of sweat; belts carrying traces of voracious dentition; booklets, notices, videos that one would think had been through the dishwasher and in which a little man takes a full ten minutes to scale a wall that any contractor would level with his wrecking ball; a mousepad, medals, statuettes, cigarettes! Houdinismokes! To smoke them is to escape! And off we go, to the mezzanine . . .

advertising blood

Open the door, Harry, the Chair is there, at the end of the hallway, awaiting you.

If there is a hallway leading to the bottom of one's self, it's this passage of bricks which Harry took for the first and only time that Sunday evening in the year 1910, while his wife Elizabeth, that lazy parody of a mother, waited in the car—and as he stepped across the threshold of Huber's Ha'Penny museum, he felt her little rat's eyes, sensed the gray trickle of her breath, and stiffened under the moist claw of her kindness. She would wait, like a mother awaiting her whore-addicted son, trusting in uterine disappointment but somewhat angered by this sudden and filthy intrusion of the Other into the cycle of the Same, vaguely disgusted at the idea that a Chair can uproot a man from his Foundation.

Open the door, Harry. At the end of the hallway. She's there.

He carried the usual hodgepodge in his pockets: padlocks, keys, copper armbands lined with pins, smutty cards with pull-tabs, tiny sticky chains, dry petals, and also the excessively protected photograph of a redhead swallowing a saber made of sugar (a saber? maybe not).

Open the door, Harry.

And when he had opened it and entered then reshut it he leaned against it, without noticing the poster, which covered three-fourths of the top panel and which he saw only hours later when his wife, at the top of her droning voice, dragged him from the well of ecstacy in which he was splashing about:

> **GRAND THEATRE,** MONDAY DECEMBER 1910 FOR SIX NIGHTS, DOORS OPEN AT 6-30 AND 6-45, THE ONE AND ONLY LADY MASTERPIECE, **EMPRESS,** THE CLEVER LADY OF MYSTERY, IN HER WONDERFUL & STARTLING ESCAPES, INCLUDING ESCAPE FROM POLICE HANDCUFFS, PACKING CASE, AND STRAIGHT JACKET, THE ESCAPE FROM THE STRAIGHT JACKET AND PACKING CASE PERFORMED IN FULL VIEW OF THE AUDIENCE—ALSO THE GREATEST SENSATION OF MODERN TIMES—*** THE WATER MYSTERY ***—ESCAPE FROM AN IRON TANK FILLED WITH PADLOCKS WHICH MAY BE BROUGHT BY ANY MEMBER OF THE AUDIENCE. ONE OF THE MOST DARING FEATS EVER ATTEMPTED BY A LADY. MUST BE SEEN TO BE BELIEVED. SOMETHING NEW EVERY NIGHT.

And the Lady at work, in siren's lamé studded with sapphires, already curved in an inverted k 2/3rds swallowed by a trunk festooned with chains, her smile imperfectly cauterized by an expression of astonishment, or of ecstatic idocy, one breast nearly bared, the other pear-shaped and receding, and at her crotch, where the right thigh crossed the left, a hinted shadow, less triangular than lozengular, a half-open bulge.

She's there, Harry. At the end of this hall. Open the door, she's waiting for you.

She was waiting for him, a twice-broken silhouette, a dim-witted Moloch of wood, folded a first time at the level of the pelvis, at her padded hips, into the double parallel horizontals of the forearms tensed in fists for armrests, so that the strong thighs and flattened ass form a support; then a second time, the knees gush out in the vertical descent and flow to the feet, a muscular foundation grafted rather than nailed to the floor.

You wanted her, and she wanted you, too. Remember. Two years ago, you wrote me a letter, you told me, Huber, dear and great Huber, I learned that you had brought back from Auburn penitentiary the electric chair that served for the execution of William Kemmler, in 1890, the first, the only, the original, the one and only chair. She's for you, Harry. I offer her to you, she offers herself, to you, take her, Harry.

These squared-off legs, of a wood at once young and gnarled, the tormented and patient grain of this wood, like restive railway sleepers, chary of fire and yet defiant of it; this hieratic back, of a disquieting breadth, as if the vertebral column placed against it had the duty to widen out and spread, as if, each man seated there, each animal fitted into it, each fury of unsettled form (and, possibly, of the least structured astonishment) went to seat itself there, had to, wanted to, aspired to stretch the pulmonary locker so as to better fit this crepuscular throne; this was what he had been trying to find since the beginning: the end.

For years the Chair had haunted him. From here on out, Howard goes to it like an incontinent man to the toilet, his only brain-wipe being his bundle of hastily-scribbled notes. Admittedly, Howard slaves away, and slaves away hard, but these posterior sessions last for ever, and conjugal duty, already at a low point, feels the effects. Sometimes, after a prolonged visit to the mezzanine, when he lies down without making either a sound or a faux pas, something comes to pass, passes, surpasses them even. Bess feels something like tiny whips lapping at her husband's thighs, the sheet pulls rhythmically away from his sweat-pasted back with a sucking, sizzling noise, she thinks she can make out a vague blue halo in the half-light of their bedroom. Howard snorts like a maniac, muscles still creased with rage and frustration. So Bess plays half-dead, on guard in her sleep, slowly mastered by a virtuoso cramp which reminds her of her first menstrual terrors; she stirs, in the way one shifts a trunk, a suitcase, Howard has to hear this troubled wildcat's noise, he clenches his thighs, one hand padlocked on his sex, and turns his back on her.

Bess stretches out a hand, which she quickly withdraws. Howard's body, though so close, seems inaccessible, insuperable, the warmth he emits has nothing of that soft aura which brioches give off when taken out of the oven, it's the core of a reactor, of fear as well.

This shit, Bess remembers, started six months ago, on a Friday.

That day, a truck with the coat of arms of the Redux Truck Co. stopped right in front of the Hordinary residence. Sound of worn steel, a slamming door, a manhandled tailgate, a box pushed inconsiderately into the middle of their drive with, stapled over the spurned warning HANDLE WITH CARE, a big brown padded envelope addressed to the name of Howard Hourdinary (sic).

It contains a document, typewritten:

THE DESIGN OF AN ELECTROCUTION SYSTEM INVOLVES THE CONSIDERATION OF A FEW, BUT VERY SIGNIFICANT, REQUIREMENTS. VOLTAGE, CURRENT, CONNECTIONS, DURATION AND NUMBER OF CURRENT APPLICATIONS (JOLTS). FIRST, THE SYSTEM SHOULD CONTAIN THREE (3) ELECTRODES. THE HEAD SHOULD BE FITTED WITH A TIGHTLY FITTING CAP CONTAINING AN ELECTRODE WITH A SALINE SOLUTION MOISTENED SPONGE. IT IS THROUGH THIS ELECTRODE THAT THE CURRENT IS INTRODUCED. SECOND, EACH ANKLE SHOULD BE TIGHTLY FITTED WITH AN ELECTRODE, CAUSING THE CURRENT TO DIVIDE AND GUARANTEEING PASSAGE THROUGH THE COMPLETE TRUNK OF THE SUBJECTS BODY. USE OF ONE (1) ANKLE ELECTRODE INSTEAD OF TWO [2]) WILL ALMOST ALWAYS ENSURE A LONGER

AND MORE DIFFICULT ELECTROCUTION. THESE TWO (2) ANKLE ELECTRODES ARE THE RETURN PATH OF THE CURRENT. CONTACT SHOULD BE ENHANCED BY USING SALINE SALVE OR A SPONGE MOISTENED WITH A SALINE SOLUTION AT EACH OF THE ANKLE CONNECTIONS. IT IS OF THE UTMOST IMPORTANCE THAT GOOD CIRCUIT CONTINUITY, WITH A MINIMUM AMOUNT OF RESISTANCE, BE MAINTAINED AT THE ELECTRODE CONTACTS. FURTHER, A MINIMUM OF 2 000 VOLTS AC MUST BE MAINTAINED, AFTER VOLTAGE DROP, TO GUARANTEE PERMANENT DISRUPTION OF THE FUNCTIONING OF THE AUTOMATIC NERVOUS SYSTEM. VOLTAGES LOWER THAN 2 000 VOLTS AC, AT SATURATION, CANNOT GUARANTEE HEART DEATH AND ARE, THUS, NOT ADEQUATE FOR ELECTROCUTION, IN THAT THEY MAY CAUSE UNNECESSARY TRAUMA TO THE SUBJECT PRIOR TO DEATH. FAILURE TO ADHERE TO THESE BASIC REQUIREMENTS COULD RESULT IN PAIN TO THE SUBJECT AND FAILURE TO ACHIEVE HEART DEATH, LEAVING A BRAIN DEAD SUBJECT IN THE CHAIR.

DURING ELECTROCUTION THERE ARE TWO (2) FACTORS THAT MUST BE CONSIDERED: THE CONSCIOUS AND THE AUTONOMIC NERVOUS SYSTEMS. VOLTAGES IN EXCESS OF 1 500 VOLTS AC ARE GENERALLY SUFFICIENT TO DESTROY THE CONSCIOUS NERVOUS SYSTEM, THAT WHICH CONTROLS PAIN AND UNDERSTANDING.

Generally, unconsciousness occurs in 4.16 milliseconds, which is 1/240 part of a second. This is twenty four (24) times as fast as the subject's conscious nervous system can record pain. The autonomic nervous system is a little more difficult, however, and generally requires in excess of 2 000 volts AC to seize the pacemaker in the subjects heart. Generally, we compute the voltage at 2 000 volts.

It was Leuchter's prose, recognizable among thousands, because there were a thousand others like it, over a hundred thousand others copied exactly, endless reproduction of the absolute polish of dead prose, and not only dead but obsessed with the thingification of the slightest vibratory particle, not the slightly frigid language of the entomologist or of the formula jotter, but that bloodless prattle which is achieved only by sheer force of inner anaemia and patient exterior scrubbing.

Alfred Leuchter[1] the small man with sophomoric glasses seemed really and truly to have disappeared into the scenery: changed into a tree, roots in the air, he had to scrape the sky to collect samples, which he would analyze so as to prove the non-existence of Paradise, his ears nevertheless crammed full of the sound of the trumpets of the Judgment of the Supreme Court. Ever since Alfred had been adopted by the Holocaust deniers, ever since he went off to Polish ground to demonstrate that the gas chambers couldn't have existed because the Nazis were incapable of making them work since they were lacking the knowledge of which Alfred Leuchter was the sole trustee in this lowly world of incompetents, ever since Alfred had licked out the swasticka'd messkit of the hounds of purity, Howard had told himself that a little discretion wouldn't hurt his reputation.

So Howard Hordinary stored the box in his cellar and wrote down in his notebook: "Gift from Leuchter to Howard Hordinary." Then he changed his mind. A sharp and black line rectified the jotting: ~~Gift from Leuchter to Howard Hordinary~~ and a more generous, bolder entry falsified: Gift from Huber to Houdini – 1910.

There. The Chair was entering into its houdinian legend and it was for the better. They give you a bone and you, you stick it in a completely different skeleton, you wedge the femur of this one into the pelvis of that one, you insert red words into a black mouth and it has to work, has to speak, whatever does or doesn't occur, a sort of habit, a custom, the garments of the living over the flesh of the dead, or the opposite, it doesn't matter, the important thing is that the grime tastes like soap and the squalid appears polished.

That evening, as an exemption, Howard paid homage to Bess. When the former came to lie down at her side, instead of becoming a tree trunk sunk in mud or a statue wallowing in sand, instead of playing a child switched off under the maternal lampshade, he crept toward her, deployed his fingers and her folds, buttressed against her a lot of little desiring bridges, running sawing bypassing, with each groaning debut combed flames, wove chains, brought the weight of his shoulders back on the armrests of Bess's withered arms, pressed the box of his stomach to the suddenly burning stone of his wife, raised her thighs in two perfect right angles, and made it last, last, last, aligning the unalignable with the unaligned, wallowing in slow motion in hollows that one would have thought sealed with torpeur, making the dried froth foam up with conviction. Did Bess appreciate it? Hard to say, to grasp, so much did the noise of her breathing match that of the rubbing of the skin and the creaking of the bed.

Rather than making her come, Howard decided (without really having decided anything) to lead her astray into a maze of sensations; he turned and overturned within her fears until then concealed in the staunch sack of mystery, practiced horrible diversions, amazing bypasses, all this time thinking and chewing words that she couldn't pick up, trusting only to the vibrations of his torso, to the lapping of his thighs, to his frozen grimace in the dark. Soon, he even doubted that Bess was there, under him, concealed by his strength; very quickly he felt all the tools of Sam's box of tricks enter into fellowship, all those butcher's cunts connecting up. And Bess didn't come: she saw, literally, as one sees the headlights of a train after a tunnel

come not closer but really and truly move away, her coming taunted her, the head of a pin hurtling down the hallways of the body, and the more Howard slaved away, knocked, bleated, the more the nail of the cry went back down her throat and pierced her lungs. In the end, she gave up, yielded, wanted to swallow him in turn, but her hands were pushed away and held against her sides, her thighs immobilized by the knees of that thing which, from then on, no longer had any connection to the Howard she knew and despised, this thing which was swarming with a hundred coiti interrupti, a thousand sacrificed joys. Sensing the defeat of Bess, unconsciously anticipating it, Howard pushed the depravity further until it offered a scrap of ecstacy, a long seminal signature of rash design that he diverted
just

in

time.

New session. His flesh finally electrified, strapped married dedicated to the chair, his penis wedged where it needs to be, Howard smiles, this'll work.

The current is alternating, just like the surges of his muscle fibers and the panting of his nerve endings. Howard holds fast. Until then, memories fluctuate, gladness follows regret and, in her bedroom upstairs, Bess must debone newspapers so as to feed the flesh of her album, piles of typographical shavings are strewn on her bedspread, her glue-covered fingers sort classify mutilate, her formerly ringed fingers nurse the dark album of clippings concerning the Great Punitive Roasting (GPR) which is happily rampant still in more than a dozen states / . . . one seriously wonders if humanity doesn't pay too dearly for instantaneous destruction (1890)/Alfred Leuchter surely knows more about the technology of the electric chair than anyone else (1990)/sometimes the prisoner catches fire, especially if he perspires too much (1991)/a thin thread of white or dark gray smoke can sometimes rise from the top of the skull or from the leg to which the electrode is affixed (1930)/young monkeys behaved exactly like children; as soon as they felt the current they cried out and appeared to endure a thousand sufferings, and when the electrodes were removed they seemed stupefied and there were even three monkeys who removed them themselves and examined them (1889).

In the mezzanine, the electric throne seems to rock on itself. Howard gives a cry that immediately chaps his lips. His hands tear into themselves. The whites of his eyes are inked very methodically with changing shadows, and the little destitute flux of blood that flows through the piping of his veins bounces along.

Tense in his Chair, Howard bawls out the name of:

~~Szuszu~~

Comes to pass, then, what happens only when the current happens to pass through him and the impulse is found.

Howard starts to ape and whirl the void, he becomes the great ape armed with stainless steel who brandishes the erect silk in honor of the aenemic tribe—suddenly, coupled bound houdinied to his Chair, he gives himself over to the bitter current which passes through everything, a blurred flux buoys up his immensely elongated cock, which bows and snorts and moves forever away from the hidden root from which it springs; what it flees is only obviousness and trickery—hullaba, sabbath, pitch.

The Chair swallows him like saliva does sand, he ensnots himself in its fibers and finds himself catapulted in mid-electric circus, into a hideous menagerie/slaughterhouse in which all sorts of galvano-bestial experiences take place, the Godhison Electric Slaughterhouse or something like that. Here, lighter than an excremental particle blown in a gust of wind, he is finally allowed to see elegant pachyderms, which, according to the general opinion, extract boundless pleasure from the electric current which torpedoes them, ecstasied congealed screwed, from trunk to asshole penisfied titillated, their massive *membrum* deafly beating time, *toumb-toumb-toumb,* within their gaze a softness! a folly!! a reverie!!! a mirror in which all the frustrations of the electric executioners dissolve. Next charge down a phallanx of mastiffs who, all without exception (Maltese, pug, bulldog, pointer), once past the first half hour, give such evident indications of rabies that they have to be trepanned without delay for the purpose of thorough examination. Then comes the turn of a trained seal [seal # 1, please!] who, hide dried out and flippers stiff, salutes & palpitates like a high tension line swelled with an unreasonable amount of energy before gnawing through its restraints and leaving the laboratory in search of a possibly briny puddle in which to die with dignity.

Howard can't believe his electrodes! This bass-ackwards journey is taking on interesting dimensions, and he wonders what fate is reserved for him in this magnificent parade. Trumpets reverberate. A red carpet sticks its tongue out along the wood floor, immediately flanked by laboratory assistants in black livery—??—!?—

Thus moves forward the inaugural Baboon the 1st, who, after having struggled like (and better than) a maniac, bites the mauve and digital flesh of Dr. Southwick (well well, it's started again, we're in Buffalo, in 1887), tearing to shreds his gray overalls, *rriahhhh!!!* but he is brought under control—an assistant manages to slide between his long fangs a sponge soaked in vinegar [another sponge is jammed under his paw, but his horny palm tears it apart through wild friction], *shriiik-za'ham!* the first jolt tears howls out of him, which seem suddenly excessively arrrh-tiiii-kew-laaate to the witnesses gathered together in the winter house of the illustrious Barnum Circus—the twenty-eighth battery component is vigorously affixed to the hairy martyred body, and the rage of his Excellence Baboon the 1st inscribes a sonorous and ascending arc which ends in a crackling shower, a mixture of infantile jeremiads and primitive supplications—the fourth electrode forces the ape to mellow and settle down, his flesh adapts and is soiled with a pungent smoke as if a dirty gust of orgasms had gotten the better of his rutting pain, he seems dazed, shaken between the similar effects of a corked wine and of unjust toil, his fangs overlap his chops like nicotined fingers on the threadbare armrest of a Chesterfield chair—barely weaned of his straps, see how once again he slips on the heinous and pinkish outfit that he only took off against his muscle's will, he crashes into furniture, slaps spectators, chattering mimicking flogging the air like anything goes. Then . . . *ouch!* forward somersault, backward somersault, the baboon climbs onto the chandelier and shits in the soup, before being shot by a—POP!—bullet in the—*schouuup!*—(pink) ass—

Clack-ee-snap!

For Howard this is the signal: fangs planted in his lower lip, ass thicketed with pain, peri-anal bald spot in full bloom, bars pushing out where the vertical slats of the Chair back are superimposed, phalanges cackling like latches eaten away by blood, vocal cords passed through the marlin spike of warbled howling, thigh muscles overheated under the lopsidedness of atrocious elasticity.

In a still poorly defined dimension, but one which is certainly neither that of dream nor that of hallucination, Howard starts to tear to shreds straitjackets unbleached as sails, jumps from wall to wall and from vision to vision, already he hears the jungle perforate the inside of his organs with its echoes, feels fear quiver in his eardrums which electricity has butterflied open like kidneys under the tripe dealer's knife. Panicked, he hammers, claws the wood of the doors and the leather of the sofa . . .

Clack-ee-snap!

The curtains piss sap, vines gorged on a bitter liquid thread their way through the patterns of the wallpaper, the windowpanes flake under the pressure of his reflection and grow dark, then form stagnant ponds where, very cruelly, shapes explode, all fleeting, obliterated by green, brown and clay-red, channels of fire plough up strips of a floor that blisters and splinters, a furious mud oozes and smokes, splashes and tears itself to pieces, two eyes pierce with their split tips the froth which gives way and dissipates in lazy islets—*///—aahrrr!* here he is, a baboon, baboon for nothing, good-for-nothing baboon, flung into the muffled paradise of deceased apes, here he is, chatting; *aarhh!* those fucking bastards drove me back to the reclusive ends of the jungle, when, springing up from behind a gigantic tree trunk, a Man—christened "explorer" by those who themselves have never traveled up any river except the menstrual isthmus of their babymaking factory—entwined me with a thousand lassos thrown whirling, then dragged me between the rotten stumps and the spiders' nests to the European cage where stale corn and sparse water, galvanic rule and policed laughter, awaits me—*i remember,* I dismember, the boat sails, the hold is dark, I deliver all through my vomit, the poorly raised African worm, the dew on the flowers too quickly lapped up, through my behind everything goes out, held balls saturated with dusk, damp wood shavings, insipid bark peelings in which the sun swarms, the boat pitches, the hold is cold, sometimes men sporting ridiculous teeth come teach me humility with metal bars, I am offered as a spectacle of the evidence of my dereliction, of my vexed rutting, I piss and spit and claw, I SAY: tear apart those pink vials which contain somehow or other the obscene marbles of your eyes, let that irritating fluid serving you in the place of blood spurt out and capitulate forthwith, because it is time—high time!—that we BABOONS achieve a bloody revenge, *slurp-ee-slurp,* that we, the baboonized in the flesh, impose our hard and hairy politiks of the extermination of man, our final solution by which all those who articulate will be backed against a wall and will finally gulp down the foolish sediment of human silt—and see it suddenly debaboonized by the high court, violently deprimatized, a leather cord winds itself around his neck and strangles the last impulses of his greedy glottis, the darkness crushes him under its canopy, a cross is raised within him, death to the left life to the right the cry above the fold below—he no longer knows which baboon he is and flees, what ba what boon what well and good baboon in him saw it, nor what oblivion raised to the second power was his—slurp-ee-slurp—!—that's it, I am learning the b-a-ba of **BABOON,** they can bring me the female, the howler, the squealer, I smell her hole and her violent attitude, around me she growls and moans, her two eyes dampen, her mouth fumes with rage, her nostrils flare, one would think she wants to mate right on the cot where I'm aping deadness—/—

Clack-ee-snap.

Seated in his chair, HH holds in his fist the drops of sweat, which escape between his fingers and design shiny time zones on his thighs. The earth revolves quicker than does his blood.

Houdini refused to let them come in. Outside the door of his dressing room, students of escapology trembled with admiration, begging the master to open up for them. They had just learned that their idol was going to perform a new sort of escape: tied to an electric chair, Houdini had to free himself from it before the current reached his limbs. An authentic executioner—the very one who was going to deal with Sacco & Vanzetti—had to make sure that the Chair functioned perfectly. Fraud was impossible. The room was packed.

But no! He wouldn't part the shutters of the Red Sea to let all the fugitive apprentices who swore only by his name & his renown come in. He wasn't of the Hebrew tribe, his blood was Egyptian, he was a fakir, a pharaoh, he was the embalmed man unjustly Italianized by the i grafted to the Houdin of mister Robert, he was the assassin of Robert-Houdin, the Hindu denied by ***SZUSZU***, the twice-denied of his father Rabbi Samuel Weisz, his father who had insulted prince Erik, had defied him and fought against him before fleeing to London and embarking for New York, where Ehrich was born, where his mother delivered him, but not there, not in Budapest, not in Hungary where already they were burning the—**crlc crlc crlc**—born in Budapest the 24th of March 1874, under the forever unwritten name of Ehrich Weisz, from which was removed the terminal z to the advantage of a redundant s by immigrato-administrative will before the h in Ehrich in turn jumped ship and a guillotining k came to dismiss the c and the h which ligatured his name, upon which he became Erik Weiss, the great Erik Weiss of Ellis Treasure Island, the Rabbi-Golem expelled from Budapest, the flying vampire of Hungary whose single bite would semitize the littlest Aryan, the cherished son of the mother-hen, his mother queen of the shackles of the flesh, Cecilia Steiner Weiss, wife of Rabbi Mayer Samuel Weissssssssssssssss—**crlc crlc crlc**—his name is Harry, Harry Houdini, he was born in Appleton, Wisconsin, America, where he married Cecilia Bess—*singsingsingsingsingsingsingsign! sing me a song!!!*—Bess? Bess? very slowly the current bellows and pumps in the stagnant water of memory in lukewarm spurts, Howard/Harry struggles in his electrodes, the vast gray pinnas of his ears are rimmed with fire, the four paws of his violence anchor the immoderation of his fury, he raises the post of his bifidate trunk before planting it in the plug manufactured by Godhison, suddenly the mastodon shines, his tusks attracting lightning, the megaphone of his cells launches the freaktacular call, releases the epileptic summons: enter enter enter enter ENTER **ENTER!**, and you will see the female with quadruple breasts and her nursing quadrupeds, you will see the stammering ventriloquist and the padlocked hercules, the bloated skeleton and the plaiter of steel, and you won't see, no, you won't see what the hand of How—of Ehr—of Houdini does when, coupled with stitched to tortured by his chair, he commands his carcass: the penis (then but only then) rears up, stamps, harnesses itself to the stomach and to the stomach speaks, soliloquizes like only the penis knows how to soliloquize, in waves, currents, spurts, shrinking then opening in a dome & bursting dribbling iridescing, under the twill straits of the straitjacket which keeps him in place, to start over is just to start, 200 volts now and more if that isn't enough! isn't enough! isn't enough! isn't e—

Into his chair attached to the weak current, strapped lashed tied, capped by the bitter sponge, the conch of his eyelids craquelured with incandescent veinlets, the casing of his nerves swollen with sparks, Houdini toppled, motionless, Houdini furioso muttered one *two three* and lowered the lever in a gesture so slow that each electron seemed set in a bubble of mercury, the current drifted away in a cadenced wave and, despite its growing exhaustion, conserved intact the memory of all the other bodies trespassed by the chair—Houdini passed by there, that which passed by there passed him by, all came to pass as if it passed by where those who trespassed had passed, to that chair also strapped tied lashed, hundreds of mutts and dozens of apes, horses and cows, a whole hecatombal menagerie subject to the voltaic whip, and the more the amperage grew the more the animal farce seized **HOUDINI**, stuffing him gutting him, the more things burned, sizzled, within him, not only his body hair, not only his hide, but also, but still the tiny stick bundles of affect, obscene thoughts crackled whose ashes no science would collect, he was no longer anything but a moist tissue balled up and too tightly knotted, a sack of tatters which steamed and went up in acrid smoke, his thighs stiffened, each muscle engorged with panic-stricken electrons which were all looking for a way out, which went and came and came back without ever finding rest, his arms dreamed of rising and falling, his legs of pumping and quickening, **ALAS!** they were numb levers, rusty, disconnected from the central processing unit, the diodes of his eyes displayed strange 000O00 zeros 000O00, which went on to bloom in spirals that were red then white then red then white, his lips retracted, uncovering scalded gums, his caudal ossicle telegraphed nevertheless two or three salacious thoughts to his penile antenna which then swelled and stood up, houdini sweated houdini bled houdini oozed, he became the young Francis beaten by his parents who, the 19th of February 1893, crawled across a field before grabbing with both hands an electric cable which, rather than healing him of being badly treated, reduced him to the state of a senile nonentity, he became Mary, the virgin of Buffalo, mated by accident with Dr. Bodie's Dynamort, and whose hymen started to sparkle like the legendary Kohinoor diamond and who was saved *in extremis* from total paralysis, little Mary who searched for the whole of her existence for the mammal capable of resisting the sparks that burst out between her thighs each time her menses subsided, HH became the cow of Galvani's nephew and disciple, professor Luigi Aldini, or rather its head, severed, which widened its nostrils and stuck out its tongue before an audience of nobles, opened its eyes, perked up its ears, became Thomas Foster, the hung assassin whose galvanized fist reared up, threatening, threatening, threatening, but threatening what? no one ever knew, Thomas Foster was no more than grimaces torsions scanscions of his own hide, was no more than that, was hardly more, houdini made a face, was no more than dumb waves and grim twitches, sunk in a bath of potassium silicate and copper nitrate, the solution to all solutions, life begun again prior to life, Houdini's life no less than any other's, the forever widowed life of Houdini chained handcuffed straitjacketed to his chair, delirious man submissive to the psychiatric whip, face veiled in leather how to suppurate one doesn't know what grating smile, in pain he had looked for the memory looked for the memento of all that sleep had robbed him of he had found the monkey the cow the walrus the elephant and the dog and the bitch, and Bess, yes, and his wife, with his sold-off mother, their two livid heads getting excited like those wheels that the smallest thing sets in motion, with pain and the memory of this pain, when he thought pain he spoke and thought of something other than pain, he thought and spoke of what you couldn't escape, the voltaic battery of mediocrity always more deeply sunk into the asshole of the dynamo of distinction, the hook of the commutator gently driven into the flesh of the continuous lie—

Huber's Chair hummed in the half-light while the procession of admirers chanted his name. Some hours earlier, two young men, Samuel J. Smilovitch and Ernest Whitehead, had been admitted by the master and had insisted on pummeling his stomach with their fists, following Houdini's assertion that he had succeeded by the power of exercise to change his abdominal muscles into bricks. The eighth punch proved fatal. Ruptured appendix. Peritonitis.

—once the lever is lowered all begins again: the current returns to its source, the electrons flake away, avoid one another, under his skull bits of magnesium congregate in a clot of orange fire, which swells and contracts before being sucked up into the slit of his pupils, *slot—slot—slot,* his lymph stops coagulating, sparks are bedding down on his skin like a blue-gray comforter, the marbles of his blue eyes scrape the inner walls of his eyelids, his fingers tarantulate, stiffen, his joints loosen and snap, a little urine dribbles the length of his left thigh and snakes around his ankle before cooling on his heel, his chest rises up, from the bottom of his lungs words climb, rustle in his esophagus, climb his trachea, the mucous of his mouth dries, his jaws crash like white-hot cymbals, and suddenly Harry expresses himself with a strong Central European accent, which throws itself like marbles into the gears of his American sentences (made in Wisconsin 1874), his four limbs are firmly held to the Chair by leather straps upon which are henceforth engraved a succession of letters: **H O U D I N I**—the lever lowered, the hand to be dealt again, the date of his birth and the place of his delivery, the ectoplasm of his father and the slime of his mother, the continuous and discontinuous current, Edison and Westinghouse, the state in the middle West and the State in the center of Europe, the place of the brother and that of the wife—in the electrical night his body opens up, leaps, flees, in the night of electricity cascades of bodies penetrate and agitate, thirsting for mutilations, iridescences, initiations, a mass of badly spoken tongues gone off to lynch all that moved around his lips, the German of Budapest like the English of Appleton, the murmur of the Cabbala and stage lingo, in the electrical night the swallowers of swords and of many other things suck him to the very root, torpedo him, bleed him, they make three meter long whips dance, whips which scissor the air and leave on the skin omegas, which vinegar sets off and makes weep, everywhere are only pleasures and Chinese tortures, the holes of padlocks moisten, chains sing, a scarf crushes his occiput with its silky knot, the straitjacket ex—

Summoned, Harry's body calls ***SZUSZU***. But see how a memory pinches off his aorta and how his throat closes up to the point of being no more than a fist, ten clenched fingers on the fluted stem of his stopped breathing: end of November 1915. Jack London was with his wife, Charmian. Houdini burned himself at the stake of public opinion, in Oakland, under the aegis of the Keith-Orpheum. He spoke to the couple about his enchained leaps into the rivers of Europe and America.

Harry, Jack asked, what do you feel when you hit the water?

You don''t hit the water. It's the other way around.

Charmian rolled her eyes heavenwards, but Houdini felt her knee against his own. Two tired animal muzzles. Wood waking up.

Harry, you don't understand, what I wanted to know, it's . . . the fear of dying in the water, by water . . . or with water . . .

You've had too much to drink, Jack, said Charmian.

You know, Houdini chained on (his specialty!), you only think about continuing to bulge your torso and tense your muscles, then emptying yourself of all your air and going slack so as to give play to the chains. And then seizing the key slid into the horny flesh of your heel . . . true contortions indeed.

Charmian burst out laughing. Champagne spilled from her glass and beaded on her wrist. Harry licked it off with his eyes.

Harry, you never want to . . .

What, Jack?

Charmian leaned to spit the pit of an olive out into the saucer to her right. Harry conjured it away even before it had touched the porcelain and swallowed it.

To give up, to accept.

To accept what?

Water.

Water?

He's waiting just for that, said Charmian, emptying her goblet.

Three days later, he tried to corner her in the hallway of her house. She pushed him away but promised him the moon (hers) if Harry would accept the challenge thrown out by Rahman Bey, the fakir who was making headlines with his prolonged immersions in a coffin which was itself submerged in water. Harry accepted.

Shit! That's how a crooked fakir forced him to play at being buried alive. Yes, an Egyptian fakir who wasn't even Egyptian, a piece of pharaonic filth answering—woof! woof!—to the name Rahman Bey, no more rahman than bey obviously, *for he was Italian,* and was called Falsetto Falsetti or some tune in the same key, cairo crapster or neapolitan neopepper, no matter, he would ridicule him under the nose and in front of the face of the impotent sphinx who served as his impresario, Hereward Carrington, that ersatz barnumesco just barely worthy to wipe Jumbo's ass.

O, Rahman Bey, I have a grudge against you, I'm going to skin you and pierce the cruel walrus of your vanity, because I, HH, have been submerged many times in coffins at the bottom of urban rivers, always escaping them while under the cyclopean attention of cameras and popular expectation—and you, cold-blooded dervish, you want to distort my record, shuffle the cards of destiny and redistribute them in your own way, force me to not run away from those boxes and chains anymore, but to hold, hold back the air, and stay remain endure, swallowed under horrifying hectoliters. But I'll do it. I'll do it for Charmian.

And Harry did it. First of all he puffed out slowly and conscientiously his 26,428 cubic inches of air during 70 minutes in a coffin in the back room of the Boyertown Burial Casket Company. Then came the 5th of August 1926, the day of the challenge thrown out by R. Bey, and this time Harry let himself be closed into a coffin containing 34,398 cubic inches of carbon-dioxide enriched air and was submerged in the luxurious swimming pool of the Shelton Hotel, at the corner of 49th Street and Lexington Avenue, in New York.

Fifty minutes later, his respiration was breathless. He also realized water was seeping into the coffin. He thought again of the story Lovecraft had written based on his drafts for the magazine *Weird Tales:* "Imprisoned with the Pharaohs." He repressed a nervous laugh imagining that scoundrel Rahman Bey stretched out beside him. Then he lost consciousness.

He came to in a padded cell, duly straitjacketed in heavy canvas. A man was standing before him, who looked vaguely like Lovecraft but smaller, and with strange glasses, seemingly soft.

Hello, Harry. How are you doing? I am Dr. Bodie. Walford Bodie. We are going to heal you. And to do that we're going to turn to ducking, which, perhaps you know, was practiced already in Epidaurus. Pliny tells how Asclepiades had invented hundreds of different types of baths, the principle staying the same, and here I cite medieval medicine: "to make one lose strength and forget fury." Faithful to my predecessor Van Helmont, I assess that the only thing you must see to is to submerge the sick suddenly and unexpectedly into water and hold them under a very long time. There is no reason to fear for their lives. This method should delight you; you, the king of the maniacs. I have followed your exploits for a long time and have naturally enough come to the conclusion that you suffer from a very distinctive form of alienation, which I will permit myself to baptize "restraint mania." Since the beginning of your career you have continually personified the figure of the maniac: handcuffed, straitjacketed, enchained, shut into a box, a barrel, a cage, what else do I remember, imprisoned in various cells, walled up . . . I suspect sexual dissatisfaction, you don't have any children, do you. I've heard of impotence due to too long exposure to X-rays—your brother is one of the pioneers in that field, I've heard. Be that as it may, your restraint mania pushed you recently to reach a threshold that I will qualify as highly symbolic since from here on out you'll practice your immersions in a coffin, and this time the challenge no longer consists of your accomplishing one of your brilliant evasions, but of defying death. It's a question of a critical stage, and it is advisable to stop you from going beyond it. That's why, Harry, we are going to heal the escape artist in you through duckings, so as to reverse, if I may say so, the direction you're pursuing.

He was led into a badly lit room where he was asked to move forward on a gangway, which overhung a vast pool many feet in diameter. At the end of the gangway, a chair awaited him; he was made to sit in it and was carefully tied in. Dr. Bodie then activated a mechanism and the chair started a slow rotational movement, at the end of which Harry found himself head down, above water that was, in all likelihood, iced. He stayed thus suspended more than fifteen minutes, and when the blood had flowed back up enough in his brain another mechanism was activated which brought about the brutal immersion of the upside-down chair in the pool.

The operation was repeated a dozen times, and it was the same for the three months that followed.

Harry heard a bell ring. Where did this sound come from? He remembered the swimming pool, the coffin, the challenge, Charmian, and decided that an hour and thirty-one minutes was more than enough. Doctor McConnell, who had witnessed the exploit from the first preparations, helped him extract himself from the coffin covered in galvanized steel, kept watertight by thirty-two screws.

When he called Jack's wife the next day to find out if she had read the papers, a servant told him that

Charmian had gone to Australia the night before. Had she left a message for him? Yes. What?

Escape. For me.

Balanced on the parapet of the bridge, Harry prepared to carry out his final feat. He was descended, it is true, from a long dynasty of imposters: petty monarch of evasion weaving in the fog of the ether their amniotic memories disemboweled ventriloquists with stammering intestines throwers of mental knives evaders of riddles & hymens famous lunatics in restraining girdles, in galvanized chains, all the more so for having been screwed into a cruel rotating armchair bound for the medico-legal moon twisted dwarves in the bellies of trunks lined with velvet and edged with brocade, rich in locks and steel chains freakish digesters of bolts and beer human beasts hurled into surprise water cures or struggling in the husk of a thick twill straitjacket whose sliding sleeves cut into their crotch and muzzle their asses and continued on to be pinned just this side of their nape, there where the reasoning buckle will reach quite soon.

Reflected in the cloudy papyrus of the water, he distinguished, gathered behind him on the American Death Bridge, the witnesses of his deferred agony, their organs magnetized by his immanent dive.

He closed his eyes and held his arms out horizontally, the squat cross of his carcass letting itself attain through mesmerism the silt below—outside of himself, he prepared to jump, once more hindered, once more linked to this tempered steel oath for which he had lost the key.

The water bristled up with gray foam and fell back down again in black hollows, its icy call rang out in the fog, he wasn't going to put off diving in for long. His chains were a snake in love with his shoulders, they imprinted an X on his torso and formed bracelets on his wrists, the waves rubbed themselves against the piles of the bridge, the wind was loaded with miniature syringes that kept on inoculating him against fear, suddenly he bent his knees and soared. His fall lasted three seconds: the first was a shout formed from three syllables cut into the silence, the second a name spelled to death, the third a saturated voice which formed a fist and smashed the waters, which exploded in a double lip that immediately curled up, it was finished, it was beginning.

Nineteen seconds, that's how long he gave himself to break through the surface again and flourish his freed hands, nineteen seconds, but until then everything had to be started over again, everything had to be dealt out, the place of his birth, Appleton Wisconsin United States versus Budapest Hungary Central Europe, German Jew or redneck Yank, continuous or discontinuous current.

Fifteen, fourteen, thirteen seconds.

He sank down like an i, like the i in Houdini that propped up the shameful Houdin, passing through and passing back through the twinned orifices of his handcuffs, seven seconds, six seconds, from the folds of his palm his nails extracted a twisted pin, five seconds more and air would be no more than a bad memory, the hair pin of ***SZUSZU***, no, of Charmian, no, of ***SZUSZU***, *shit!* he no longer knew, four seconds, he inserted it into the padlock's lock and lay in wait for the magic click, three seconds, two seconds, one second life forever over.

Last night's session had cleansed him of all aspirations. Three short-circuits in less than an hour, Howard couldn't stand it. This morning, he tried to improve the chair's generator, but of course he was missing certain indispensable components; he called one or two retailers in town, each time they answered him with *delay, delivery in a week, no that model no longer exists.* Howard ended up hammering on the fridge, there he is, sprawled on the couch, the television broadcasts a report on the nuclear crusade of a mediocre American president, assassinated or reelected, it isn't very clear which, the beer grows warm as quickly as the ideas in his head, he picks up the telephone, dials Leuchter's number, a polished voice tells him that no messages will be taken for the whole month of August.

Someone rings the doorbell. It's Shelley, the neighbor.

Hi Howard. Bess isn't in?

Shelley enters his living with an overbearing stride and starts to nose about from one room to another, running a red nail over the dust of the armrests and an expert eye over the bottles piled beneath the sink. She wears a roomy and yellow dress, which shows off silly smiles under her armpits and leaves a white mark on the upper portion of her breasts, a mark which could be exciting if it didn't remind you of Batman's or Mickey's stylized bangs. Howard ogles her without blinking, quite relaxed. When she comes back to the threshold, from which he hasn't moved, something has changed in the house. The brasswork of the lamps, the texture of the carpet, the outline of the furniture: on all of it, rather absurdly, has settled a slightly obscene veneer. He looks Shelley in the eyes, reads them like a flip-book made from the end-stubs of checks: all the outstanding sex checks forming strata, a wad of too long neglected ardor.

Bess has gone to buy meat. For a few moments, Howard imagines her stretched out inside the Plexiglass conch of the case, labeled all over, graded weighed assessed, marbled with *$$$*, while a butcher in a white hat, indifferent to her charms, Roy or Clem, cuts trims debones, then slips two fingers into her vaginal operculum and with a nimble rotation of the forearm expertly undoes the entrails, before passing the flame of his Bunsen burner over her skin, neither too close nor too far, each hair scorched to order, and there's Bess's head, eyes half-closed, eyebrows silky and tongue cooked, eying the just-unfrozen broccoli one case over, no, his wife deserves better than this, she deserves the vows that he has vowed to her, the more or less metaphorical knees which have come to ground at the foot of his conscience, future projects which no architect of their destiny wanted, and those thousands of muffled declarations, which the eyes thumbtack into the eyes before vinegar gets the upper hand over wine, but what does it matter, the more it rots, pickles, sours, the more it dies out, the more all that which should have taken root, grown, flowered, lazes around in them, that's how the immense venison stench spreads out, that's how all the sparks bundle themselves up in a crude bundle with which one can hardly whip the ass of events anymore, giddyap darlin'!

With his chin, Howard indicates to Shelley the driveway from which is missing the couple's Buick. The woman shrugs her shoulders and cut&pastes herself into the living room. She works her ass into the patterns on the sofa and opens a random magazine on her knees, upon which are still visible the imprint of the tile floor that she shined. Already the grillwork is vanishing, but Howard's gaze can't stop coming back to it as if it were the creases of sheets on a cheek, lines graphed on paper. Impossible, though, to see past this lattice.

He closes the front door and comes to sit down five centimeters away from this tall blond.

All right, Howard?

In Shelley's voice, the end of a nerve looking to be pinched.

I heard you're doing magic tricks. Like that other guy, Houdini. He was Italian, wasn't he? I saw the film with Tony Curtis, he's crazy that stiff, you do that same sort of stuff or what? What a lucky devil Bess is, she doesn't have to be bored stiff every day every day every day every day every day every day every day . . .

An airplane cuts through Shelley's words, which are immediately guillotined by its engines, then spat back out far away, very far away—like birds reduced to feathers and shreds—into another urban metastasis, where other ears pick them up, dilute them in the silence.

Howard doesn't answer at all, because the only response that he could give just came up in his throat, like water forced backwards into a plugged siphon, and his brain alone sponges it, filters it, incorporates it with the other ditties, mixes and remixes it until it flares up in eyes already badly irrigated by alcohol: yes, Shelley, yes, and magic is filthy, magic is monstruous, what did you think, you didn't listen to the news at noon, they've executed one more, Jess Joseph Tafero, unless it was Wilbert Lee Evans, or Derick Lynn Peterson, at the Virginia State Penitentiary, or in Florida, they replaced the elephant ear—yes, Shelley, that's what they call the piece of sea sponge placed in the cranial electrode to stop the flesh from scorching—they replaced it with an artificial sponge but obviously those morons didn't realize that this synthetic and cavernous big liver, even saturated with saline solution, would reduce the current at least a hundred volts and would gently torquematize him, even that simpleton Frank Klingo, the chief doctor of the prison, has said it, the execution proved "hardly attractive on the aesthetic level," but okay, Tafero, or Evans or Peterson ended up dead, and tomorrow it will be our turn, you'll see, at us too they'll hurl stronger and stronger televised jolts, commercials more and more soaked through with incompetence, recklessness, and we'll remain like oxen at the start of the last century, under the watchful eye of cleavers then of pneumatic pistols, they are allowed to roast our occiputs—

How about a good fuck? asks the image that

Howard makes Shelley into when he opens his fifth Bud.

Do I want to fuck you? But of course, answers Howard's hand, while closing on the nape of Shelley's neck.

Cut the crap, Howard.

He could show her two or three things, relics, posters, handcuffs. He could make her laugh, pull coins out of his nostrils or scarves from his ears. He could chat her up, have her visit the mezzanine, show her the Chair. He could sit her in it, reassure her, start with very weak jolts. He could—

Noise of gravel being awakened by rubber, burning smell of a motor, which coughs, then nothing more. Schlack of a tailgate being raised. Outside, Bess puts the icebox down on the driveway and shouts his name.

You too will go through this yourself one day Shelley.

Bye.

Sunday morning, boiling cup of coffee and raspberry-filled donut, Lucky lit, pumped more than smoked, on the doorstep, blackbird on the alert in the eaves where the leaves have formed a paste, not the slightest dew, a balky lawnmower quite near, which coughs, a fan of spat-out clippings coming over the fence, a dog pushing the *Daily* with his muzzle, a faraway radio, piping, turned off, door bangs. Howard has to go, he goes.

I'm taking the Buick. Did you hear me, Bess?

Yes! Don't forget to bring her some cookies. You know how your mother likes them.

Tie knotted, underpants pulled up and balls cradled, he crosses the living room. Chair rejected, perspective straightened out—he crosses the threshold and slams the door. The doorhandle of the Buick is burning hot, Howard lifts his eyes: the sky is Microsoft blue and the sun full of suspicious spots.

He knows the road that leads to the nursing home well, it pays out, then climbs, then snakes, then goes along and finally comes down, seems to disappear so as to better climb again and once again meander, and all this time his body is imprinted with these awaited movements, all this time his hands, his thighs, his joints know the forces that will weigh on them, know that to fit the road which leads to his filial duty is also to condemn his body to the worst of trajectories, one which transmutes each grumbling molecule into a servile electron.

He knows the moment when he will park, the moment when he will cut the motor and lay his head on the steering wheel while closing his eyes, the moment when he will lift his head and extract the key from the ignition, scratch the side of his nose, the moment when his left hand must land on the handle of the cardoor and push, push downwards all while shoving with all the strength of his shoulder, and then the air will come into the compartment of the car, the air will smack him like a not very fine fish who escapes from the net and flops on the dock, *like a fish on the dock,* he will put one foot on the gravel of the drive, and the first thing his gaze will frame will be the sliding glass doors which will open as soon as he is less than 20 centimeters from them, then he will have to go past the reception desk where, perhaps, very certainly, a nurse will be leaning over a register, before which, probably, but not necessarily, another relative will be shifting from one foot to the other, he will see only the man's back, his hair, and he will continue on, to the elevators, he knows the floor, he knows the hallway, and the smell, and the open doors of the rooms, the wheeled trays with their lukewarm glass of water and their framed photograph.

When Howard saw the bed where, degraded, his mother, tucked in, was dying, he gagged; she brushed this away with an unringed hand, as if to say, come on, Howard, you thought I was enrolled in Resurrection 101 or what?

❀

If he had ever wanted to kneel it was that day, at the end of the bed, numb, at her mercy, but he did better, from the tip of his lips he let drip a long, orphaned kiss which went off to wither the sparse veins still stretched out on her languid flesh, and said, but like a prayer: if I come back tomorrow, what bond will still unite us? hearing which of course she stayed silent, drawing on the wall of her false night the sketch of a frock that one frowns when one drowns, sabbath hullaba pitch, but finally mother what hope what armor what drunkenness tempts you down here, so low, sabbath, and she answering him like one cancels out a life, with great fragmented gestures, come on, Howard, my hullaba, my pitch, what what what? you didn't know? and he bending his knees, making kneel so much within him too many things so that none among them dares lift head or tail, so you didn't know, all my life for all my life and for all the time the story of those men one calls erect (and of thosewomen who aren't called anything, who are forgotten) has lasted, I fought, fought in my own way, shamefully unhappily gently unbearably incidentally unbelievably insignificantly uselessly everlastingly, I washed the dishes of ghosts and made the beds of monsters, I opened the mail of the dead and drew up the announcements of some while holding at arm's length the expectations of others and the tiny hopes of a third group, yes, by way of ironies absences presences, forgettings as well, come here, closer, by way of armfuls of nothing concealed in the pretty myriads of everything, attentions, measured terrors and parodied declarations, in my own way I fought but not so as to see you on your knees, certainly not, your knees are only the hinged portions of that body that I gave built cut measured designed for you when you were still only a desirous assault in your father's eye, when you were still and above all only a love egg come into my already bloodstreaked womb where so many men in their own way had, going beyond their rights & their duties, decided, on top of me, what they wanted from me and what they didn't want from me, didn't they, you give birth only to what you hope to bring safely through childhood, and if there was a child who was desired as much as dried up at the orifice it was you, and know that your mother has never repudiated the insane pyrotechnics of her first period, never, I simply folded everything in two then four then sixteen, drained each molecule of blood, you'll understand and you'll see because you too will lose your skin and bang against those bones which are underneath, you hear me Howard?

Howard had started to play with the remote from his mother's bed, pressing now the north button, now the south button, now the east button, now the west button, forcing her to fold and unfold, sitting her up sitting her up again, making her into the recumbent figure of his nightmares or the seated figure of his dreams. Thus several minutes drifted away, fully cadenced by the ricochets of the sun off the metal bedrails, the shifting of shadow on the tiled floor, the waves of sound which slipped in from the hallway. Emily didn't dare tell him to stop, all these imposed movements intrigued her, awoke memories, quarrels, frolics, after all it was her son, it had been an eternity since she had seen him having fun, fiddling with buttons, trying to make something work.

Howard put the remote back on its stand and looked at his mother, tilted at a forty-five degree angle, clutching the side rails.

If you really want to please me, she finally said, get out of here and walk a little bit. Walk for me.

That evening Howard gets a call from Sam. He gathers a few dollars from the dish in the entryway and leaves, taking care not to slam the door.

He pulls away in the Buick, in the direction of the *Bright Angel Bar.* Past the last houses, the road thins out between the hills, from time to time torn open by dingy headlights. Howard's car still smells like a cheap cut of meat and, on the passenger's seat, crumpled tissues and a tube of lipstick bounce with each lurch. It is ten to midnight. Howard shoves a CD savagely into the CD player, and "No Queen Blues" by Sonic Youth starts to cut through the reeking car. Howard thinks again of the baboon, of the rage that visited him. Blisters are still budding on his forehead, and his teeth burn his gums so strong is the desire to bite through them and come back to tightly buckle his jaws. Fucking monkey! It isn't by climbing trees that he'll get back to ***SZUSZU***, wherever she is. You are unworthy of Houdini, he howls, unworthy of your mother and your wife, *unworthy of the Chair!* A hundred meters in front of him, a lightning bolt bursts out of a stump and for an instant lights up the whole valley to his left, so violently that the network of mauve and red gleams stamps a blinding checkerboard onto his retinas. No matter how hard Howard rubs his eyes, everything in front of him is no more than squares, rectangles, lines set off by a vivid margin. He accelerates while "No Queen Blues" climbs in force and in resonance, each riff lancing an abcissa and each no no no no no an ordinate, imposing thus on Howard a more definitive trajectory, forcing him to push the speedometer needle into unexplored territory, to invent a sixth, a seventh gear, so that it is no longer the Buick being catapulted in hairpin leaps along the bends of the hillside, but a mixture of Howard, alcohol, music, exhaustion.

A sign explodes on the right, the gravel spits out from under his tires, he brakes, backs up, just right, the ᗺ of *Bright Angel Bar* imprinted in the neon blue steel on his hood.

He takes the key from the ignition and sucks on it a moment, emptied out. The car radio now broadcasts something syrupy by Dean Martin.

When he enters the bar, the TV screen suspended above the pool table shows a crowd standing about in the rain in front of high walls, waving signs with dripping messages before the inquisitive camera eye, but it isn't necessary to listen to the off-camera voice, smudged by the conversations of the customers, to understand that it's the umpteenth protest against the death penalty, somewhere in America, and that for a few hours lethal injection or the electric chair will allow the newspapers to double their print-run, and judges to triple their shot of whiskey when they come back home in the early morning.

A Coors.

Bud is half price tonight, throws out the brunette squeezing out a sponge above the sink.

Thanks, Jill. A Coors.

He waits a good ten minutes before swiveling on his stool. Above the pool cues, a photo of Tiger Woods decked out with a bleeding hole in the center of his forehead, with, a little higher up, the caption: **GOLF WAR: 1 DOWN.**

When Howard emerges from the *Bright Angel* an hour and forty-three minutes later, Sam Turnpike is waiting for him in the parking lot, behind the bar, accompanied by someone he has never seen.

You took your time getting here, Sam lets slip.

Howard stares at him as if looking at an old geographic map. He recognizes certain borders, certain depressions, but not the mauve cove of excitement at the level of his gums. Sam has his feet turned inward, he rocks slightly forward then backward, and his hands seem to be searching through his pockets for keys that don't exist. The other guy, who keeps in the background, seems to be speaking to a cockroach that must have taken up residence under the collar of his wrinkled shirt.

Well? asks Howard.

As usual, Sam doesn't answer right away, and is satisfied to massage that part of his body which he assumes is more loquacious than his lips. Three years ago, before the accident, Turnpike swore only by the wood he himself worked, and the fact is that the wood knew the least of his failings, beech especially, which had taken less than three autumns to define the ball-less wonder that was Sam, beech so resistant in its knots but so sketchy in its branches, and so lazy in winter, beech had immediately felt under Sam's palm the congenital absence of perserverance, and the bark let itself be cut without resisting out of fear that Sam would discover in its fibers the too exact reflection of his destiny. Then the blade got stuck in a knot, Sam had insisted, the chain had given way, the chainsaw kicked out. Twenty-three stitches, eleven pins. To help him limp on even six feet under.

Where's the girl? Howard then asks.

Let's go, suddenly announces the stranger.

Howard, meet Ed. Ed, this is Howard.

Sam Turnpike's mobile home seems gathered on itself and its mysteries, its big ass of planks and paneling spitefully seated on foundations which smell of piss and dead raccoon. Sam unlocks the door and goes in first, followed by Howard then Ed.

In the half-light, it is hard to make out the girl. She is stretched out on the bed which occupies a third of the space, next to undone sheets; she seems absorbed in solitaire: the only thing heard is the noise of the cards, as card touches card.

Sam throws a switch and the neon of the ceiling light releases a white pool over the girl's body, which immediately seems to stick to her skin. She is nude, except for green panties and a pearl necklace.

The one called Ed approaches her, speaks to her in a low voice for a moment, nods his head, then gets out from underneath the bed a wooden box from which he removes various implements: a sort of transparent tube ending in a copper knob carrying the inscription **MASTER HIGH FREQUENCY UNIT,** four plastic armbands covered with aluminum foil, a gauze bandage. Then he finds his way to the kitchen nook, pours a little water into a pan, adds to it a handful of salt.

Howard lights a cigarette and sits next to the T.V. set, on a stool. Sam doesn't take his eyes away from the other guy.

Ed immerses the gauze in the warm and salty water, then cuts off four lengths of it, which he attaches around the ankles and the wrists of the girl. The latter squirms slightly but keeps her eyes closed.

Ed pulls out a rectangular case from under the bed. Sam takes hold of it, half opens it, smiles, then pulls out two hundred-dollar bills from the back pocket of his pants and slips them to the guy. He undresses clumsily and sets about fastening the strange object contained in the case onto his semi-erect member. Seven rings of decreasing size bound together by leather straps. A red wire comes off the bottom, and Sam connects this to a little battery that he fastens with adhesive tape to his back, just above his buttocks.

Ed bustles about with the transparent tube, which he coats with a substance similar to resin. He presses the button at the base of the shaft and the tube starts to buzz and emit sparks.

Static electricity, thinks Howard, who has started to rub his crotch without realizing.

Sam stretches out on the girl and sets about penetrating her. At first, she grimaces, but very quickly the lines of her face congeal into an indecipherable expression, her mouth opens wide and she tightens her hands on Sam's thighs. Ed leans over her and wanders the fluorescent and vibrating tube over the tips of her breasts. At one point the girl rears up, her head goes backward and the nape of her neck forms an arc, the muscles of her calves and thighs bulge and one of her armbands comes free with a dry crack. Sam kicks out. He lets out a shout. It's over. Ed takes his place and shows Sam, who seems drunk, how to use the tube.

Ten minutes later, it's Howard's turn.

Not being circumcised, he experiences some difficulty getting the seventh circle around his glans. Ed tells him that the sensation will only be stronger.

When Howard stretches out on the girl, he experiences immediately a familiar prickling. He closes his hands on her hindered wrists and looks her straight in the eyes. Ed comes near and holds out the tube to him. Howard seizes it and makes it come and go on the girl's thigh, then slides it slowly between her buttocks.

Then something attracts his gaze: the game of cards with which the girl was playing solitaire when they arrived. All the cards are blank, but in appearance only, because in tilting his head slightly Howard can distinguish on their faces a whole series of minuscule blisters, geometrically arranged goose bumps, that only the tip of a finger could read. Braille.

Howard nevertheless introduces half the tube into the blind girl's anus. He's going to come. No, it's not come that is forcing its way through his cock. Howard is afraid, and fear is going to make him pee, right there, on the girl, between her legs, in front of Sam and Ed.

Immediately his salt-impregnated urine finds a circuit with the copper connections that join the armbands. It is too late. His pupils dilate in fits and starts through seven spheres, seven cylinders inserted into one another: that of fascination (1) inserted into that of oblivion (2) inserted into that of illusion (3) inserted into that of escape (4) inserted into that of slow death (5) inserted into that of the greatest cold (6) inserted into that of—?

Howard finally knows what the seventh circle is. He rushes into it with a leap, with a jolt, with a bolt of sperm, long and jerky, the hoop is broken, flames spurt out, he clutches the girl, staves her in, goes through her and houdinizes her, then escapes in a brutal blossoming of electric flesh and blood.